Rent a Third Grader

by B. B. Hiller

Illustrations by Meredith Johnson

LITTLE APPLE

SCHOLASTIC INC.

New York   Toronto   London   Auckland   Sydney

ISBN 0-590-40966-2

24   9/9 0 1/0

Printed in the U.S.A.   40

First Scholastic printing, September 1988

For my favorite
fund-raiser,
Mother.

Chapter 1

The Beginning

Brad Carter wasn't about to forget the day Rent a Third Grader really started — although nobody knew it at the time. It was the first day he didn't have to give his social studies report.

Miss Bilgore's class was studying Communities. Everybody in the class had to do a report about one part of the community. Brad's report was on gas stations. As far as Brad was concerned, there was nothing wrong with gas stations except that his father owned one. Brad was sure he was going to look as dumb doing a report on gas stations as Melissa Jefferson had looked doing a report on convenience stores. She'd even brought a can of soup into school for the report. At least Brad didn't have a quart of oil to show the class.

But he had everything else. His father had absolutely loaded him down with stuff from the garage. He had given him a monkey wrench, an instruction manual for installing power windows, an air filter, and ten road maps. They were out-of-date road maps from before the interstate highway had been built. His father said he could give them out to his classmates. Melissa had given everybody in the class little packets of salt and pepper. Brad threw the maps into the garbage on the way to school.

Jennie Everett was doing the report before Brad's. Her report was on the Police Department and neither of her parents worked there. (Her father was the president of the town's bank.) She'd gone to the Police Station with her father to talk to the police officers. She told her class that the police had showed her the jail and they'd even locked her in it.

"It was terrible," she said. "I made up my mind right then and there that I'd never commit a crime." She smiled sweetly. A few of the kids laughed. The idea of Jennie committing a crime was very silly. Jennie Everett never even chewed gum in school.

"And the police loaned me these," she said, holding up a pair of handcuffs. "And this," she announced. It was the key. "Here, I'll show you how they work." She convinced Miss Bilgore to hold out one of her hands. Jennie flipped open the unlocked cuffs and snapped one on Miss Bilgore's wrist. Then she clicked the other cuff onto the back of Miss Bilgore's chair. Miss Bilgore tugged to show that she really was locked in, and she smiled all the while.

"Now, where did I put that key?" Jennie asked. Miss Bilgore stopped smiling. "Maybe I put it in this pocket. . . . No, then I guess maybe this one. I *thought* I had it right here." Everybody had been

watching Jennie put the handcuffs on Miss Bilgore. Nobody had seen what she'd done with the key. Just when Miss Bilgore started getting annoyed, Jennie announced that she'd found it. It had been sitting on the chalk ledge the whole time. Then everybody knew she'd been teasing. She unlocked the cuffs and freed Miss Bilgore.

"Ta-*da!*" she said. Everybody clapped. "Now, who wants to volunteer to help me with a demonstration on how police officers use their nightsticks?" Everybody laughed.

Except Brad. He just glared at the monkey wrench and the air filter, which were in the bag next to his desk.

Chapter 2

—◆—

Saved by the Bell

Things started looking up when Jennie began talking about Partner. Partner was the Police Department horse that Officer Chambliss rode. All the kids knew Partner. Officer Chambliss was the afternoon crossing guard and Partner was always with him. Sometimes the kids brought carrots or sugar lumps for him. Brad liked to pat his soft nose. He didn't like to give him things to eat because the horse sort of slobbered when he ate. Still, he was a nice horse, and Jennie was having a good time telling the class about how the police took care of him.

Brad looked at the clock. Their reports were supposed to be ten minutes long. He'd clocked his four times last night. It was eight and a half minutes. He'd have to talk really slowly. So far, though, Jennie's had gone on for twenty-five minutes and she was still going strong.

She really got a kick out of standing in the teacher's place and being the center of attention. As far as Brad was concerned, she could stand up there all day. As long as Jennie was there, he wasn't. He leaned back in his chair happily.

" . . . and Officer Chambliss feeds him three times a day. He gets hay and oats and, in the hot weather, he gets extra water. And that's the end of my report." She flipped her right braid back over her shoulder with her left hand and smiled.

The end. Brad could feel a very large lump in his stomach. There were ten minutes left in the period. That was just enough time for Brad's report. He had to do something. Fast. Jennie was walking back to her desk.

"I have a question," he blurted out.

But he wondered what the question was.

"Yes?" Miss Bilgore said.

"How old is Partner?" he asked.

"I dunno," Jennie shrugged.

Nine minutes and fifty seconds left. Still too much.

"Does he belong to Officer Chambliss?" Brad asked.

"No, he belongs to the Police Department," Jennie said. "And when Officer Chambliss retires to Florida next month, they're going to sell him."

Now, *that* was interesting.

"Who's going to buy him?" Brad asked.

"I dunno," Jennie said.

Nine minutes exactly.

"Boy, he's really a neat horse," Brad said, struggling. "Did you get to ride him when you were at the Police Station?"

"Nobody gets to ride him except Officer Chambliss," Jennie said.

"That's not true," Louisa Appleby interrupted. The class looked at her in surprise. She seemed surprised, too. Louisa Appleby almost never spoke in class — or out of it. "I rode him," she said.

"No way," Jennie contradicted Louisa. Jennie was good at sounding like a total know-it-all. Brad felt sorry for Louisa.

"It's true," Louisa said. "I rode Partner with Officer Chambliss when I got lost one time in the parking lot at the Southbrook Mall. Or was it the time I got lost at Firemen's Carnival?" She seemed to be talking to herself. "No, maybe it was when my little brother got lost — or maybe both times. . . ." Her voice trailed off in thought.

Somehow it didn't surprise Brad that Louisa spent so much time getting lost. She was the most confused and fuzzy person he'd ever known. One day she had come to school wearing one blue sock and one white one. He could understand blue and maybe green if her bedroom light bulb was burned out. But blue and white? Today, her socks matched, but they drooped. And her frizzy blond hair was a mess, as usual. It always seemed that her hair was as confused as she was.

"It was two times I rode Partner," Louisa announced finally. "When I got lost and when we were looking for my brother."

Eight minutes.

"You know," Brad said, really digging now. "If I were going to ride Partner, I think I'd most like to be on him when he leads the Founder's Day Parade. It would be neat to have all those people watching and to know that everybody was following me. And he always looks so shiny then. Do you know how Officer Chambliss makes him so clean and shiny?" Brad asked Jennie.

Much to his relief, she did. And she told him. And the rest of the class. Right then, Brad was really glad for Jennie's fabulous memory. She remembered every single detail, from the hoofpick to the dandy brush. She just kept on talking. Seven, six, and then five minutes were left. He'd done it!

When Jennie finally sat down, Miss Bilgore checked the time. "Oh, dear, Brad," she said as the bell rang. "I'm afraid we're going to have to ask you to wait until tomorrow to give us your report. I hope you don't mind, but Jennie's report was so interesting that I just lost track of the time. I guess you did, too."

"Yeah, I did," he lied. Then he put the paper bag with the materials for his report back into his cubby.

He looked at the clock again. Twenty-three hours and twenty minutes until the next social studies class.

Chapter 3

————◆————

Louisa Speaks

The next day was the second time Brad didn't have to give his social studies report.

Before the social studies period began, he carried the bag from his cubby again and sat, full of dread, waiting to be called to the front of the room. To keep his mind off his misery, Brad thought about other things that made him miserable.

He thought about Jennie. Jennie Everett always did everything right. She always did it best. Her homework was never late. Her papers were never crumpled and smudgy. She never tore her clothes. Her smooth brown hair never pulled loose from her tidy braids. The ribbons never fell off the ends of the braids. Grown-ups thought she was cute.

Brad hated her.

Then he thought of how unfair things sometimes were. It was unfair that he was the last one in the class to give a report. It was unfair that his parents had made him do the report on gas stations. And it was mostly unfair that his report followed Jennie's.

The bell rang.

"Miss Bilgore, Miss Bilgore!" Louisa was standing and waving her hand in the air. "I saw Partner yesterday!"

"We all saw Partner yesterday," Jennie told her. "He was at the crosswalk, just like always."

"I know," Louisa said, and sat down.

"Was there something special about seeing Partner yesterday, Louisa?" Miss Bilgore asked. She seemed to be trying to be extra nice to Louisa to make up for Jennie being snotty. But even if everybody in the class were extra nice to everybody else, Brad thought, it still couldn't make up for Jennie.

"Yes," Louisa said, standing up again. "I thanked him for helping me that time I got lost. I patted his nose. It was soft, like velvet. I gave him my carrot sticks left from lunch. They were soggy, but he liked them. When they were gone, he looked for more and when he saw that I'd given him everything I had, he kissed me." She sighed and then sat down.

There was silence in the classroom. Nobody had ever heard Louisa say that much at one time before.

Jeremy Gingrich broke the silence. "Arf! Arf! I've just been kissed by a horse! Eeeeeeyiuuuuu!" Nobody laughed.

"Jeremy!" Miss Bilgore spoke sharply. "You know, class, Louisa has reminded me of something I wanted to talk about. That is the idea of people helping each other — doing good deeds for each other — in a community. It's a *good* thing about communities. Helping others is a way of thanking them for helping you, isn't it? Can you think of times when somebody has helped you?"

Later, Brad thought it was odd, though he was never sorry about it, that all the examples everyone gave had to do with Partner. Somehow, the image of the horse kissing Louisa made everyone re-member how neat he was, and so they wanted to thank him.

Rob diMarzio told about the time Officer Chambliss had ridden Partner over to where he'd fallen off his bike and then helped him up and washed his scraped knee at the water fountain until they learned it wasn't badly cut at all.

Melissa Jefferson told the class that when Officer Chambliss "parked" Part-ner in front of their store, more people always came in to buy things.

Alison Carey told about the time her dog had run away and how Officer Chambliss had found him and brought him back, riding on Partner. Ever since, the dog would bark at other horses, but not Partner. They were friends.

Zoe Chessman remembered the time some bullies tried to steal her camera. Officer Chambliss and Partner chased them away.

Ellie Vanquist said her favorite story about Partner was that he was the very first thing she ever saw in the town the day her family moved in. He'd been with Officer Chambliss directing traffic as they drove in.

Brad had had enough of this. He'd known Partner all his life, but the horse was just a horse and, as far as Brad had known, he'd never done anything heroic. But he felt the eyes of his class upon him. He had to do something. So he told a story about the time he'd left his lunch bag near the crosswalk — he'd been shooting marbles there before school, see, he said. Then, by the time he remembered what he'd done with his lunch, Partner had gotten into it. The horse had eaten his sandwich, cookies, and apple.

"Are you sure about this story, Brad?" Miss Bilgore asked, her voice dripping with doubt.

"How could I forget it?" he challenged. "I got to go home for a second lunch, and it took so long that I missed square dancing! I tried to get him to do it again the next week, but, see, he'd gotten smart about my mom's deviled ham sandwiches, see?"

Brad knew Miss Bilgore didn't believe him, but she laughed, so he figured he wouldn't be sent out of the room the way he'd been the day he put the rubber snake on the floor by Miss Bilgore's desk.

After he'd told his story, somebody else told a really boring story about Partner. Brad thought it was a big lie, but Miss Bilgore seemed to be interested, so while she was listening to it, he shoved the paper bag with the material for his report under his chair.

Then he heard the most wonderful sound in the world. It was the bell. They'd spent the entire time talking about Partner. They hadn't spent any time at all talking about gas stations. Class was over.

Brad scooped up the bag from under his chair and put it back in his cubby, hoping Miss Bilgore hadn't seen it — hoping she'd forgotten it — permanently.

And tomorrow, he thought, maybe there will be a fire drill. They hadn't had one in a long time. Now that the weather was warm, it might even be the kind of fire drill where they walked all the way out into the school yard, not just to the front entrance.

And maybe the tooth fairy was real.

Chapter 4

Planning for the Future

When it came to doing good deeds as a way of saying thanks to Partner, Brad felt he had more reason than anyone else in his class. So, after school, instead of walking straight home, he stopped to pat the horse and to give him his apple. He had the apple left because he'd been too nervous about his report to eat it at recess. Nobody ever raised their grade by throwing up in the middle of giving a report.

By the time Brad got to the crosswalk, most of the kids had left school and Officer Chambliss didn't have to stop traffic much.

"Hi, Officer Chambliss," Brad said.

"Uh, hi, uh, Burt."

"Brad," Brad said, correcting him politely.

"Right, uh, Brad," Officer Chambliss repeated. Officer Chambliss never remembered anybody's name. Actually, that wasn't quite correct. He remembered something close to everybody's name. Alison was called Alice. Louisa was called Lucy. Jeremy was Jeffrey, and so on. It wasn't that he was getting old, though he *was*. He'd always called everyone in town by slightly wrong names. He even called Brad's father Jake, though his name was Jack and it said so on the gas station: Jack Carter, Prop. (for "Proprietor").

"Okay if I give Partner my apple?"

"Sure," he said. "If you'll tell me something."

Brad made his hand flat and put the apple on his palm. He offered it to the horse. He didn't want Partner to mistake any loose fingers for some delicious apple.

"Sure, what can I tell you?"

"How come all the third graders came and hugged my old horse today?"

"We were talking about him in class," Brad explained.

"Oh, yes. That girl — Ginnie — was asking me questions last week. Is that what this is about?"

"Jennie, you mean?"

"Right, uh, Jennie," Officer Chambliss corrected himself.

"Well, sort of," Brad said. "We were talking about things we really like in town."

Partner was done eating the apple. He ate everything — even the seeds and the core. Brad wiped his hand on his jeans and then patted the horse.

"Now, don't get too fond of Partner," Officer Chambliss said.

"How come?"

"He's going away soon. So am I."

"Going away? Where to?"

"A little condo in Florida. We've been saving up a long time, and now it's time to retire."

"You and Partner have been saving

up to buy a condo in Florida, and you're moving there?" Brad asked, surprised.

"No, not Partner and me. Me and my wife."

"But what's going to happen to Partner?" Brad asked.

"Oh, well, he's going — today's his last day, you know — say *kids!* Wait up there!" Officer Chambliss had spotted some second graders who were stepping out into the street.

Even though there really weren't any cars coming, Officer Chambliss was careful to be sure they were safe. One kid kept dropping pieces of an art project. Brad could tell it was going to take forever to get him across the street. Besides, he'd learned all he figured he ever really wanted to know about Partner. It was time to go home.

Chapter 5

———◆———

Mr. Mustache

Louisa always enjoyed walking to school. She could see all sorts of interesting things. Sometimes they were so interesting that she didn't get to school on time. She sort of liked days like that. Miss Bilgore didn't.

At first, it seemed like a pretty ordinary day. It was a nice walk and all, but nothing too interesting. Until she got to the Police Station. There was Partner. At first, she didn't recognize him because he wasn't wearing his saddle. He just had a halter on and a lead rope. Two police officers and a man she didn't recognize were leading him toward a truck with a horse trailer behind it. The strange man was short and fat. He had a dark, bushy mustache and bristly eyebrows. He didn't look like the kind of man who smiled a lot. He also didn't look like a man who liked horses. But he had a horse trailer, so he *must* like horses, Louisa reasoned.

Louisa had seen lots of horse trailers. People used them when they were taking their horses to horse shows, or races, or new homes. After all, you couldn't just put a horse in the backseat of a car. Louisa liked to see horse trailers on the highway. Sometimes the horses' tails would be blowing in the wind. She liked to see that, especially on hot days. She thought it might be fun to ride in a horse trailer.

Partner didn't seem to agree. He was giving the men a lot of trouble. The mustache man took the lead rope and led Partner toward the trailer. He followed patiently — for a bit. Then the man walked up the ramp. Partner simply walked to the right side of the trailer.

The man stepped back out of the trailer, looking confused.

This was just the kind of thing Louisa liked to watch on her way to school. She put her books on the ground and sat under a tree where she could get a good view.

Mr. Mustache yanked at Partner's halter. Louisa didn't like that. Partner wouldn't be happy about that and then he wouldn't do too well at the horse show when he got there. Mr. Mustache led him back toward the Police Station. Then he tried to aim the horse at the trailer. Partner wouldn't turn around. Mr. Mustache brought a carrot out of his pocket and tempted Partner into turning around. Partner turned around. Mr. Mustache gave him half the carrot and then he led him toward the trailer again. The man walked up the ramp. This time Partner didn't go off to the right side of the trailer. He went to the left. Mr. Mustache yelled at him and his face turned bright red. Louisa felt sorry for Partner.

Mr. Mustache tried to make Partner walk backwards into the van, but Partner was too smart for that. As soon as his feet got to the ramp, he started going forwards. Next, Mr. Mustache took a handkerchief and put it over Partner's eyes so he wouldn't know where he was going. Louisa had played enough pin the tail on the donkey to know that you could just about always find a way to see around the handkerchief. Partner could, too, it turned out. This time he just stopped at the ramp and wouldn't move another inch. The man slapped him. The man yelled at him. The man yanked at his lead. The man waved carrots in front of him. Even the smell of carrots wouldn't make Partner move.

"This is ridiculous!" the man said. "I'm going to go back to the plant. I'll bring the big truck over tomorrow morning. He'll get on that for sure!"

The police officers, who had been watching silently all the while, just nodded and took Partner back to his shed

behind the Police Station. Mr. Mustache climbed into his pickup truck and started the motor. Then, when he pulled out of the driveway, Louisa could see the writing on the door of Mr. Mustache's truck for the first time: HappiPet Food Company.

Pet food companies took horses away in vans for only one reason: to make pet food. Somebody was planning to make dog food out of Partner!

Chapter 6

The Telltale Pickup Truck

Brad was sitting peacefully at his desk. He was watching Jeremy Gingrich assemble paper airplanes. Then, all of a sudden, everything went totally crazy.

He could hear Louisa wailing while she was still outside the school, but there was no way to tell what she was wailing about. As a matter of fact, he couldn't tell what she was wailing about until after she had been in the classroom for some time. Miss Bilgore and all the girls ran over to her as soon as she got to the door. Miss Bilgore was going to send Melissa to get the school nurse, but the nurse, Miss Weiss, showed up on her own. After all, practically everybody in the school could tell from all her screaming that Louisa was in trouble.

Mildly curious, Brad looked up. There was no blood. She didn't look like she'd broken anything. She was just screaming. And crying. Boy, did she have the faucets turned on! About six different people handed her tissues. She didn't even see them. She just kept yelling something about a trailer and a blue pickup truck. Brad thought maybe she'd gotten hit by a truck. But she looked okay. When she started yowling about Partner, he thought she meant Partner had gotten hit by a truck. But that was nearly impossible. After all, he hadn't even been at the crosswalk that morning.

Brad tried to ignore Louisa, but it wasn't easy. He took out a piece of paper to make the kind of airplane Jeremy made. Somehow, Jeremy's seemed to be able to stay in the air longer than anybody else's. He folded it down the center. Then he folded it inwards, just the way Jeremy had. Then he —

"They were taking Partner *away!*"

Louisa yowled. "In a trailer. He had this big, mean face and a bushy mustache and this truck — and it, and it, and it — " she stuttered and didn't seem to be able to finish her sentence.

Jeremy used his thumbnail on the creases. Brad did the same thing. The next fold was another long one.

"On the side, it said . . . " She shuddered. And wailed.

Brad watched Jeremy finish up the last two folds and did his the exact same way. He was almost too busy with the folds to notice Jeremy's final touch. But Brad *did* see it. It was a paper clip. He put a paper clip on the nose of the plane. Of course! If it didn't have weight in the front, it would just sort of turn upwards and then flop back down to the floor. That was the secret. Happily, Brad dug a paper clip out of the mess in his pencil box and slid it onto the plane. Perfect.

"But he wouldn't get on the trailer! He knew! Partner knew!" Louisa shouted, almost victoriously.

Brad could hardly wait to try the

plane. And nobody was looking now, he told himself. Everybody in the class, not to mention the entire rest of the school, was standing around watching Louisa have hysterics. He glanced to be sure the coast was clear. It was. He lofted the plane into the air.

"I'm telling you, Partner could read what the truck said!"

"What did the truck say, Louisa?" Miss Weiss asked in her best there-there-dear voice.

The plane took off perfectly. It was beautiful. It soared, slowly at first while it climbed, then, when it reached the top, the nose dropped, just a little bit (because of the paper clip), and began to circle majestically toward the floor. It landed right by the classroom window. Brad went to get it. He picked it up. He glanced out the window, thinking how wonderful it would be when he could fly the plane outside at recess.

Just then, a truck drove by. It was a blue pickup truck. It had a horse trailer on the back. The driver was a mean-faced man with a bushy mustache. Suddenly curious, Brad looked at the lettering on the side of the truck.

"What kind of truck was it?" Miss Weiss asked again.

Louisa still couldn't answer, but Brad could. And suddenly he felt almost as bad as Louisa. "I know," he said. Everybody in the classroom looked at him. "It was a horse van, come to take Partner away," he told his classmates. "The HappiPet Food Company is going to turn Partner into horse meat!"

Louisa turned totally pale and looked like she was going to faint.

Chapter 7

---◆---

The Real Beginning

Louisa didn't really faint. She just fell down. She stood back up, her hysteria nearly under control now.

"We gotta *do* something!" Melissa cried.

Almost the entire class yelled "Yeah!" at the same time. And that was the moment when Brad realized that he might just have worried about giving his social studies report for the *last* time. He glanced at the paper bag in his cubby and looked smugly away.

"Of course we have to do something," Brad said. "But what?"

Now that Louisa wasn't screaming anymore, things could return to normal.

The third graders filed back to their desks and sat down. Brad remained standing. He had to stay in charge. As long as he was standing, he was in charge.

"We'll protest!" Jennie announced. "We'll write letters to the Police Department and the newspaper and the HappiPet Food Company!"

Letters, Brad thought. Wasn't that just what he'd expect from Jennie? He decided to wait for further developments.

"Who's going to pay attention to letters from third graders?" Jeremy asked.

"They may not pay attention to a letter *you* write, Jeremy," Jennie said. "But they'll pay attention to *me*."

Right on, Jennie, Brad thought.

"We can march in front of the Police Station," Alison said.

"How long would your parents let you do that?" Brad asked.

"Oh, about one minute," Alison said. "You're right. It's not much of an idea, but I don't think letters are, either, and I don't have any others. Do you?"

The moment he'd been waiting for.

"Well, actually, I have a thought," he said, sauntering up toward the front of the classroom. When he was standing next to Miss Bilgore's desk, he shared his thought. "I think we ought to save Partner."

"That's what we all think, Brad," Jennie said.

"Well, I mean *really* save him," Brad said. Jennie planted her hands on her hips and challenged him with a look that had shattered lesser men. "I think we should start a club to earn money to pay for Partner's happy retirement. I think we should all do work for the community so we can make money to pay for Partner to live in a pasture. I think this should be our way of saying thanks, not just to Partner, but to the whole town."

There, he'd said it. Everything depended on what happened in the next few seconds. At first, nothing happened.

Brad thought that was a good sign.

The first person to speak was Louisa — if it could be called speaking. "Wow," was what she said, staring at Brad in awe. Then she blew her nose.

Chapter 8

———◆———

The Election

Things started moving pretty quickly after that — faster even than Brad had expected. He'd known that if he'd jumped right in at the beginning, nobody would have paid any attention. Most people just thought he was good for jokes, but he knew he'd have Jennie and Louisa on his side, since they were the ones who'd started this whole thing. His brainstorm had worked — up to a point.

Absolutely everybody in the class thought it was a great idea for them to try to make money to save Partner. Nobody knew how much they'd need or how they'd make it or where they would put Partner once they did get the money.

Pretty soon, everybody was yelling at everybody else and nothing could be heard by anybody. Then, for a while, Brad was afraid that his whole plan would fall apart. But Miss Bilgore came to his rescue — or so it seemed.

"Class, class," she said in a firm tone of voice. "I think you have come up with a very interesting idea connected with our study of communities, Brad." He glowed in the light of the praise. "Now let's see how a community really works when its members need to work together for a common goal."

She went on for a while, but what it came down to was that she wanted the class to elect a committee to talk to the police, to talk to local horse stables and farmers, and to find out if they *could* raise the money necessary to support Partner.

Committee? That wasn't what Brad had in mind at all. He wanted to be in charge. He wanted to be the leader, the boss, the center of attention!

" . . . So, now, we'll have a vote," Miss Bilgore was saying. "Are there any nominations for the committee chairperson?"

Hands shot up all over the room. Brad was confident they'd all go down once he'd been nominated.

"Brad Carter," Rob diMarzio said. Brad beamed as Miss Bilgore wrote his name on the blackboard.

"Anybody else?" she asked. Brad couldn't believe it. Hands were still up.

"Jennie Everett," somebody said. Ugh, Brad thought. He wasn't worried about beating her, though. Lots and lots of people didn't like her at all and wouldn't vote for her for head flyswatter. Miss Bilgore wrote her name on the blackboard.

"Any other nominations?" she asked. One hand remained in the air.

"Louisa Appleby." *Louisa Appleby?* Her name went on the board beneath Jennie's.

"All right, now, everybody, take out a small piece of paper and vote for one of the nominees for committee chairperson." Brad hated the word "chair-person." He thought "chairman" was a much nicer word, particularly when it applied to him, which is what he wanted to have happen. He took out some paper and wrote his own name. He tried to disguise his handwriting so Miss Bilgore wouldn't know he'd voted for himself. Voting for himself seemed like bragging, though he was certain Jennie would vote for herself. Louisa probably wouldn't. He hoped she'd vote for him.

In a few minutes, Miss Bilgore collected all the ballots and told the class to read from their Red Readers while she counted the votes. She took the ballots and left the room with them. It didn't take long.

Five minutes later, Miss Bilgore returned, beaming. Brad was sure that was good news for him.

"We have a rather surprising, yet I think *good*, result of the election," she said. Brad wasn't so sure that was good news for him.

"We have a tie," Miss Bilgore said.

Brad was sure then that it wasn't good news for him.

"A three-way tie," Miss Bilgore said. "So, class, please congratulate your three co-chairpeople, Brad, Jennie, and Louisa."

The worst, Brad thought, standing up in disgust to accept the applause. *Co-chairpeople, indeed.*

Chapter 9

Three's a Crowd

Their first committee meeting went just about the way Brad had expected. It was a disaster. In fact, it seemed to Brad that the only thing that had gone right that day was Mrs. Stearns' phone call to the police. Mrs. Stearns was the school principal. She called the Chief of Police. He'd told her that Partner *was* being sold to HappiPet, but he'd agreed to wait for another day or two to see if the third graders could do something. That meant that the committee had to work fast.

Jennie absolutely insisted that he and Louisa come to her house after school. Once they were there, she spent most of the time arguing with her mother about skipping her ballet class that afternoon. Jennie won the argument, of course.

"Now, here are the things I'm going to do," Jennie announced after she'd sent her mother off to bring them some soda and cookies. Brad could just see himself ordering his mother to bring him and his friends a snack after school. She might do it, but then his allowance would be cut off until age 25 — at least.

"I'm going to have Daddy call the Channel Four News — " Jennie began.

"This isn't 'Daddy's' class project, Jennie," Brad said.

"We've got a job to do. Grown-ups can help us."

"Grown-ups are the ones who *caused* the problem that it's our job to solve," Brad told her. "We don't need grown-ups to solve it for us."

"We need all the help we can get!" Jennie flipped her braid over her shoulder. It was one of the most annoying things she did. She did it a lot. It was meant to look final. It did.

"Not from grown-ups!" he said, pushing his sleeves up over his elbows. He hoped it looked like he was determined to stop bickering and get to work. Jennie glared at him across the table.

"I think we should make some posters," Louisa said. "I can draw horses. I've been practicing." Both Jennie and Brad looked at her, wondering where she had been while she was sitting next to them.

At that moment, Mrs. Everett came into the room, carrying a tray with enough goodies on it to satisfy the entire class. "Here, dears," she said. Brad enjoyed watching Jennie cringe with embarrassment about being called "dears." Then he looked at the food. He was really hungry, but he didn't want Jennie to have the satisfaction of seeing him gorge on her cookies.

"No thanks," he said smugly.

Louisa, on the other hand, took a chocolate chip cookie. That was Brad's favorite kind. She ate one bite of it and left the rest on the plate right near Brad.

He could smell its delicious sweetness.

"What do you want to make posters for?" Jennie demanded, turning on Louisa.

Suddenly, Louisa's eyes filled with tears. Brad could tell that Jennie was about to get into a fight with Louisa, and that would not be a pretty sight. He interfered.

"Now wait a minute," he said, hoping he sounded like Miss Bilgore. Since neither Jennie nor Louisa paid any attention to him, he could tell that he hadn't sounded a bit like Miss Bilgore.

Jennie glanced at the clock. "Oh, it's almost four o'clock," she announced. "It's time to leave for my ballet class. You'll have to go now." That's how Brad and Louisa learned that she had changed her mind about ballet. Or maybe she had just changed her mind about the meeting.

So they left. And that was just the first meeting of the committee.

Chapter 10

---•---

Making Progress

The next morning, there was a note on Brad's desk when he got to school. It was in Louisa's spindly handwriting. It read:

> Brad: Call a horse farm.
> Jennie: Call HappiPet.
> Louisa: I'll make the posters.

Brad saw that the same note was on Jennie's desk, too. It seemed to him like a good way to divide up the jobs, except they still didn't know what posters Louisa was going to make. When Miss Bilgore asked the co-chairpeople what had happened at the meeting yesterday, Jennie announced that they'd decided Brad would call a horse farm, she would call HappiPet, and Louisa would make the posters. Nobody asked what posters Louisa would make.

That night, with a little bit of help from his mother (he would rather have died than admit that to Jennie after their argument about her father), Brad got the phone numbers from the yellow pages for five nearby horse farms and called them. The first one didn't have any room to board a horse, but wanted to sell Brad some riding lessons. His mother said no. The next one only boarded riding horses for $200 a month, thank you very much good-bye. Brad choked.

Two of the stables wanted $100 a month to keep Partner in the pasture. Better, but still way too much, and then one of them tried to get Brad's mother to buy some "aged manure" for her vegetable garden. She didn't buy any of that, either.

Things were not looking good.

Brad called the last place. It was called Akers Acres. He hadn't called them first because the name sounded so cute. He knew Jennie would love it. He spoke with Mr. Akers, who agreed to board Partner for $50 a month. He told Brad his brother was a police officer, so he'd like to help out. Brad was glad there was somebody with real community spirit. He told Mr. Akers that somebody would probably call him. Brad had done his part.

Jennie had her father call the president of HappiPet. Mr. Mustache's real name was Rodney Snodgrass. He told Mr. Everett that he was angry about the whole situation.

"I made a deal for that horse, fair and square, and I want him."

Mr. Everett reminded him that the police had decided to see what the third graders would propose before they actually made the sale. Mr. Snodgrass grumbled.

"What's he saying?" Jennie asked.

"He's grumbling," Mr. Everett said. Jennie listened on the extension phone. That's just what Mr. Snodgrass was doing.

"I'll tell you what, Everett," Mr. Snodgrass said when he stopped grumbling. "If those kids don't stop interfering in thirty days, I'm going to start legal proceedings. In fact, I'm going to call my lawyer right now!" He slammed down the phone.

"What does that mean, Daddy?" Jennie asked.

"It means you've got thirty days, Jennie. By the end of that thirty days, Partner should be well taken care of — or Mr. Snodgrass will take him for good!"

Thirty days didn't seem like much time at all.

When Louisa got home, she brought out all her poster paints and the easel she'd gotten the Christmas she was four. She put it up as high as it would go. Then she got out her paper and pencils and began to design the posters. It would take her a long time to finish her part, but she loved to draw pictures of Partner. Sighing contentedly, she began her task.

The next day, Brad and Jennie reported to Miss Bilgore and to the class. Jennie didn't say anything about her father making the call, but Brad could tell he'd done it from the way Jennie said " . . . Mr. Snodgrass told us . . . " It made Brad feel better about calling the farms by himself. His mother may have helped, but he'd done most of the talking — except about the manure. Louisa told the class that the posters were coming along just fine, but nobody paid any attention to her.

Everybody was too busy realizing how much work they were going to have to get done. In just thirty days.

Brad could picture that Mr. Mustache on the phone with his lawyer, scheming to steal Partner. It made him shiver to think about it. And that was nothing compared to the way he figured Partner would feel about it.

Chapter 11

---•---

Louisa Does Her Part

The second committee meeting was much better than the first. For one thing, it took place at school, where Jennie couldn't get into an argument with her mother (though, when he thought about it, Brad was sort of sorry he'd missed out on the cookies). For another thing, the whole class was there, except Michael Warner, who had chicken pox, and Jessica Stankovitch, who had to go to the dentist.

There was no way Brad could stop Jennie from standing up at the front of the group like she owned the whole world — any more than he could have made Louisa do it. So Jennie was in charge.

"Now, who has ideas about how we'll get the money?" she asked.

The way she'd asked the question, it sounded like she thought they'd have to rob a bank to get the money. Brad thought they could probably rob her father's bank and get away with it. But that wasn't the point, of course.

"We should have jobs that earn money for Partner," he said.

"Yes?" Jennie said, waiting for more. He didn't have any more. There was silence.

"Here's what I think we should do," Jennie said. She liked to be the only one with an idea. She gleamed.

"Notes in supermarkets!" Melissa interrupted her. "They all have bulletin boards, you know. We can put notices up there."

A few people began nodding — some enthusiastically. "Hey, good idea," Mark Hartwell said.

"Just what I was going to suggest," Jennie said. Jennie then wrote "Supermarkets" on the chalkboard.

Then they decided to put an ad in *The Penny Saver,* which was a weekly advertising paper that everybody in town got for free.

"We'll tell our parents about the project so we can do chores around the house," Alison said.

"And our grandparents — " Zoe said.

"My mother would give us some money — "

"But that's not the point," Brad interrupted. "All of our parents could *give* us money, but we have to *earn* it." He tried to sound like the guy in the television commercial who told you how hard the bankers worked to *earn* their money. A lot of kids snickered.

"But the important thing is *Partner,*" Jennie said. "So if our parents give money, we've succeeded. Right?"

It didn't sound right to Brad and it wasn't what he'd had in mind at all. "No," he said, standing up to Jennie. "If our parents give money, then it's our parents' project. *We* haven't done anything at all."

"But if we don't succeed, then Partner will end up as dog food!" Lisa wailed.

"Then we *have* to find a way to make money!" Brad shouted, punching an arm into the air as if he'd just hit a home run.

The kids started cheering and going crazy. Brad stood there, grinning. After all, the last thing in the world he wanted was for Jennie's father to give them $50 each month. Brad was pretty sure that the man could — and would — do it if Jennie asked him.

"Okay, so about this ad. What's it going to say?" Jennie asked the group.

"I have finished one poster," Louisa said, speaking for the first time.

"That's nice," Jennie said. The way she said "nice" made it sound like it wasn't nice.

"Here," Louisa said, unrolling her work. One look and the kids knew it was just what they needed. At the top, it

said: "Help us save our Partner." Then there was a really nice drawing of the horse, all dressed up. Underneath the picture, it read:

RENT A THIRD GRADER
If it can be done, we'll do it!
Speedy Service.
Reasonable Prices.
Call: 555-7300

Maybe Louisa wasn't such a flake, after all.

Chapter 12

The Work Begins

Louisa got elected to make some more posters. Ellis McIntosh got the job of putting them up around the school because he was tall.

Melissa got chosen to write the signs for the supermarket bulletin boards because she had the neatest handwriting. The four kids who lived nearest each of the four supermarkets agreed to put the notices up at each one. In addition, Melissa said she was sure her parents would put one up in their store — even though they didn't have a bulletin board.

Brad got elected to put the ad in *The Penny Saver*. That was his reward for being so good about making the phone calls to the horse farms. Rob diMarzio agreed to come with him and said they should go to his house afterwards. Rob diMarzio had a pool table in his basement. That was much better than going home to Brad's house, where there was nothing to do. Especially since he'd lost his last baseball in Mr. Costello's yard the day before.

The Penny Saver office was filled with people who wanted to get their ads in that week.

"Here," said Rob, handing Brad the form they had to fill out with the exact wording for their ad. They'd already decided to write the same things Louisa had put on her poster.

Brad took the pencil and began to write carefully. Rob talked to him while he was trying to concentrate.

" . . . and then, the next thing you know, this giant monster appears from nowhere and it's like he's really hungry and he wants to eat the spaceship. With the people on it."

Rob was a big movie fan and he never forgot a detail. *Space Attack* had been playing at the movie theater in town the week Brad had been away for vacation and he really did want to know what happened, but he also wanted to have the ad come out right.

" . . . so then, the captain — he's the one who really liked this girl space thing with the green hair — decides he has to save the ship so he can live to see the green-haired thing again."

"He really liked her?"

"Yeah, really. So just the very last second before the monster bites into the ship with these incredible teeth — "

"Next?" said the woman behind the counter. It was their turn. Brad was sorry the waiting was over.

"I'd like to put an ad in the paper," Brad said, asking more than saying.

"Let me see what you want to say," she said, tugging the form from his grasp. Brad was ready to answer all her questions about why they were earning money and what would happen to Partner. As it turned out, she had only one thing to say.

"Four thirty-three."

Brad didn't know what she was talking about. "Huh?"

"The charge is four dollars and thirty-three cents for this ad."

Money. That's what she was talking about. There he was, trying to say "thank you" to the community, and this woman wanted money. He hadn't ever thought that he'd have to pay for the ad and he didn't have any money on him at all.

"I don't have that much with me," he said.

"Well, how much *do* you have with you?" she asked.

He reached in his pocket. He already knew it was empty. Rob came to his rescue.

"Can you send us a bill?"

"For four dollars and thirty-three cents?" It was just the way Jennie would have said it.

Rob nodded.

"Minimum charge for billing is twenty dollars," the woman said.

"Okay, so run the ad five weeks in a row," Rob said. "Can you bill us for that?"

"Yes, I can bill you for that," she agreed. Then she took down all the information for the bill and told the boys the ad would be in this week and the four that followed. They thanked her and left the office.

"How could I forget about money?" Brad asked.

"It worked out okay. They'll send you a bill."

"Sure they'll send me a bill — for twenty-one dollars and sixty-five cents! How are we going to make that much money, plus the fifty dollars for Partner?"

"No problem, Brad," Rob said calmly. "When you care about something, the way you do about this horse, we'll all find a way. Boy, I think what you're doing is great. You must really love that horse, huh?"

"I guess so," Brad said, but he wasn't sure at all. He wondered what Rob would think if he knew the main reason Brad was doing it. Rob's social studies report had been on the movie theater. He had told the class they sold 563 popcorns a week. Even that was more interesting than gas stations.

"So, anyway," Rob began, returning to the plot of *Space Attack*. "When the captain sees the monster's teeth, it reminds him of that guy Jaws from the James Bond movies. So he gets this giant magnet . . ."

Chapter 13

Publicity Pays

The ad was published in *The Penny Saver* the next day. Brad saw it as soon as he got home from school. It was just full of mistakes and Brad knew they were his fault. It read:

RENT A THRID GRADES
If we can do it, it can be done.
Speedy Prices.
Reasonable Service.
Call 555-7300, ask for Misss Billgorm's clash.

One look and Brad knew that he should have paid more attention to what he was writing than to what Rob was saying. He had his mother call *The Penny Saver* and they promised to change the ad for the next issue. In the meantime, at least he'd gotten the phone number right!

When he showed the ad to the class, he told them it cost $4.33. He didn't tell them the bill would be for $21.65. He explained — as his father had explained to him the night before — that when you go into business, you have to spend money in order to make money.

That got him elected Treasurer.

Ellie, Alison, Jeremy, and Zoe reported that notes had been put up on the supermarket bulletin boards. Ellis said he'd put Louisa's first poster in the school lobby and the second one in the lunchroom. Louisa said she'd do two more in the next few days.

Then all they could do was wait.

They didn't have to wait long for the first call. Miss Mortimer, the principal's secretary, brought them a phone message before lunch. At lunchtime, Brad and Jennie used the phone in the office to call the person back.

"Hello," Brad said. "Do you want to Rent a Third Grader?"

"Huh?" the voice on the other end said.

"Rent a Third Grader," he repeated. "You called and left a message for Miss Bilgore's class about our ad?"

"Oh, yeah, the ad," the man said. "Listen, I need four hundred pounds of mulch. Can you deliver it this afternoon?"

Brad covered the mouthpiece and spoke to Jennie. "Can we get four hundred pounds of mulch to this person this afternoon?"

Jennie glared at him. "Give me a break," she said.

Brad gulped and spoke into the phone again. "I think you misunderstood our ad," he said. "We're Miss Bilgore's third graders. We do chores to raise money for — "

"What are you?" the man demanded. "A bunch of seven-year-olds?" He seemed confused.

"Actually, most of us are eight — "
Brad said, but the man wasn't listening.
He'd hung up.

"Mulch?"

"Some people," Jennie said.

Brad had to agree.

Chapter 14

Akers Acres

What happened over the next few days made the mulch phone call seem pretty exciting. Because nothing happened. Nobody called about the notes in the supermarkets. Nobody called about the ad in *The Penny Saver*. And nobody called about Louisa's nice posters.

In fact, there were just two phone calls. The first was from the Police Department wanting to know when the kids were going to pay for Partner's first month's boarding so he could be moved to the farm. The second was from the Police Department, too, saying that Mr. Snodgrass had had his lawyer call them. They *had* to move Partner as soon as possible!

On Monday, Miss Bilgore arranged a visit for the class to Akers Acres. It was really more of an everything farm than just a horse farm, so it seemed that the horses had lots of company from the other animals. Mr. Akers showed the kids the pasture where Partner would graze. It was a pretty field with lots of sweet grass (grass didn't seem sweet to Brad, but Mr. Akers assured him it *would* seem sweet to Partner). There was a nice old apple tree in the center of the pasture. Brad hoped very much that Partner would be able to live in that pasture. He only wished he knew how it would be paid for.

The whole class had a wonderful time at the farm, meeting all the animals in the barn and running in the pasture where they were certain Partner would run. In the pigsty, they met a sow named Mildred who was due to have piglets any day. She was absolutely enormous. In the henhouse, they watched while Mr. Akers collected freshly laid eggs, and they each had a chance to hold the eggs while they were still warm.

The goats had their own pen next to the pigsty, outside the cow barn. They patted the goats and the kids. Then the class went into the cow barn and took turns milking one of the cows. They each had a taste of the fresh milk, drinking from a ladle. It was warm and very creamy, not much like milk from the supermarket.

They met the other horses that lived at Akers Acres. There were four of them. Two of them were working horses and they pulled a hay wagon so the class could have a ride. The other two were retired horses, just like Partner. They seemed gentle and content. Mr. Akers patted them affectionately and allowed the class to give them snacks.

Then Mrs. Akers showed the class her vegetable garden and her orchard. She gave everyone in the class a small jar of apple jelly that she had made herself. She let them taste her goat-milk

cheese. Brad didn't like it, but he thanked her for it just the same. He was sure he would like the apple jelly.

By the end of the visit, Brad could imagine Partner in the field. He could see him eating the fresh hay and the sweet grass.

Mr. Akers invited them all to come back for another visit when Partner was there. They said they'd like that.

On the bus on the way back, everybody was pretty quiet. Brad thought everybody was thinking the same things he was. And when the bus passed a blue pickup truck hauling a horse trailer, there was a gasp. Then Brad *knew* everybody was thinking the same thing he was.

They just *had* to save Partner.

On Tuesday morning, they got their first break. Melissa Jefferson announced that she'd gotten a job. She promised she would work very hard at it and earn lots of money to save Partner. Brad wondered how Melissa had been able to manage what everybody else in the class wanted to be able to do. There was nothing extraordinary about Melissa. In fact, she was pretty normal — maybe even not quite that. So what was her secret?

It turned out that her secret was that she was working at her parents' store, which was something she did every day anyway. This time, though, her parents were going to pay her. Twenty-five cents an hour!

Brad reached for a pencil and some paper. In a few minutes, he'd figured out the good news. Melissa would only have to work two hundred hours a month to cover Partner's costs, plus another eighty-six and a half hours for the expense of the ad. That was pretty close to ten hours a day — if she didn't take Sundays off.

That didn't really make Brad — or anybody else — feel much better. Then, Tuesday afternoon, Miss Mortimer brought three phone messages to the class. Brad could barely contain his excitement when he realized that meant that people actually had jobs for them to do!

Chapter 15

Ellie at Work

Ellie nodded solemnly while old Mrs. Tooker gave her instructions. "Now, don't walk too fast. Charlie doesn't like to go too fast. He likes to sniff. And don't tug on the leash, understand?"

Ellie understood. She'd walked lots of dogs before. She wished Mrs. Tooker would stop talking and just let her do her job. Her job. She liked the sound of it. It sounded so important. Well, it *was* important. She had been selected for the first real job that needed to be done by Rent a Third Grader. She was a dog walker and she was going to earn a dollar from Mrs. Tooker every time she walked Charlie.

Mrs. Tooker was pretty old and seemed to have trouble seeing Ellie. Ellie could understand why she'd want some-body to help her walk Charlie. She hoped she'd need help practically every day. Walking Charlie was going to be fun.

She clipped the leash onto Charlie's collar and they were off for their half-hour walk. She waved gaily to Mrs. Tooker so she would know they'd be fine, but though the woman still stood at the door, she didn't seem to see Ellie. "Good-bye," Ellie called. Mrs. Tooker waved then.

Charlie seemed delighted for a chance to walk. He was well behaved, so Ellie didn't have to tug at the leash (though she wouldn't have, since Mrs. Tooker told her not to). He sniffed at almost everything — flowers, trees, grass, gar-bage, other dogs. He growled a little bit at another dog, but when Ellie spoke sharply to him, he quieted down right away.

"That's a very well-behaved dog you

have," the other dog's owner said.

Ellie explained that he wasn't hers. She thought if she told other people about Rent a Third Grader, they might get more business. The other dog's owner didn't seem interested, though, so Ellie and Charlie walked on.

The half hour went very quickly. It was almost as much fun as playing dolls with Melissa. Ellie could hardly believe it when she looked at her watch and saw it was time to go back to Mrs. Tooker's. "Come on, Charlie," she urged him. "Time to go home."

Charlie seemed to understand the word. He sniffed the air around him, decided on the route he wanted to take, and set off toward home. Ellie followed. Within minutes they were back at Mrs. Tooker's, knocking on the door.

Mrs. Tooker was very glad to see them, and Charlie was glad to see her. He wagged his tail happily and then trotted over to his bowl to lap up some water.

Mrs. Tooker asked Ellie to wait in the living room while she got some money to pay her. The room was quite dark, but not dark enough to hide the fact that the furniture was all very old and nearly worn out. Some of the slipcovers were torn. The carpet was threadbare. Ellie was sorry when she sat on the sofa because it had a broken spring and she was nearly sitting on the floor. Mrs. Tooker didn't seem to notice Ellie struggling to get up out of the sofa, and Ellie didn't think it was her place to tell Mrs. Tooker about the broken spring.

"Here you are, Ellie," she said, handing her a folded bill. "Charlie seems to have had a wonderful time with you. Can you come walk him again tomorrow?"

"Oh, yes, I'd love to," Ellie said, tucking the dollar into her pocket. "I'll be here about the same time."

Ellie was glad to be back in the sunshine when she left Mrs. Tooker's. She promised herself that tomorrow she would not sit on the sofa again while Mrs. Tooker got her dollar.

She had actually earned the dollar. That was good. That was exciting. That would help Partner. She pulled the dollar out of her pocket to look at it. Even though she knew that all dollars looked about the same — some wrinkled, some fresh — she wanted to look at it.

But this dollar didn't look the same as all the others. It didn't have a picture of George Washington on it. It had a picture of Alexander Hamilton on it. It wasn't one dollar. It was ten dollars!

The possibilities swam through Ellie's mind. First, she thought maybe Mrs. Tooker had given her ten dollars as a sort of advance. It was meant to cover ten dog walks.

Nope. If she'd wanted to do that, she would have said something about it.

Second, Ellie thought maybe Mrs. Tooker just wanted to give extra money to save Partner. After all, she was an animal lover. No, Ellie admitted, Mrs.

Tooker was a dog lover, not a horse lover. Again, she would have said something about it to Ellie.

But there was Ellie with ten dollars in her hand and only *one* of those dollars belonged to her class project. As to the other nine . . .

As if it had been planned, Ellie found herself standing in front of the window of the five-and-ten. Jennie had just bought a new Barbie outfit at the five-and-ten last week. It was a Cruise Set, with a bikini, a matching cover-up, a deck chair, and the cutest pair of sunglasses.

Clutching the ten-dollar bill in her hand, Ellie entered the store. There it was. Jennie hadn't even showed her the evening dress that went with the set. There were also some tropical flowers to go in Barbie's hair. They were Ellie's favorite colors, pink and purple.

Ellie picked up the box and looked at the price sticker. Eight twenty-five. Plus tax it would be less than nine dollars. Ellie looked at the ten-dollar bill to make sure she still had it. It seemed like a dream come true.

Swiftly, Ellie took the box over to the counter and joined the end of the line for the cash register.

It was so easy to picture her Barbie in the Cruise Set. She and Melissa could play with their Barbies on the weekend. Melissa would just love the Cruise Set. Melissa had a Poolside Set. Their Barbies would be *so* glamorous!

How nice it would be to live the glamorous life that Barbie lived, instead of the ordinary life that she, Ellie, lived. Or the sort of shabby life that old Mrs. Tooker lived. Suddenly, Ellie could feel that broken spring again. She could see the dingy living room with no lights on — probably to save on electricity. And maybe the lights didn't make any difference anyway. Ellie knew Mrs. Tooker was nearly blind. She couldn't see Ellie at the end of her walk. And she surely couldn't see the difference between a one-dollar bill and a ten-dollar bill.

"Next!" The checkout lady said. "Just this Barbie dress?"

Ellie couldn't move or speak for a minute. The checkout lady glared at her. Finally, Ellie knew what she had to do. "Uh, no," Ellie stammered. "I'm not taking it. It's a mistake. Sorry." Ellie backed out of the line, flushed with embarrassment.

Part of her was a little sad when she returned the Cruise Set to the shelf. But most of her knew she was doing the right thing when she left the store and turned toward Mrs. Tooker's house.

Chapter 16

—•—

Brad's Brainstorm

"Hey, guys, we've got to do something!" Brad was desperate. "I mean, this isn't working!" Although Ellie had gotten a job from the ad, the other two calls were both from Mr. Snodgrass. He wanted the class to know he thought they were butting in where they didn't belong.

The co-chairpeople were having a committee meeting in the school library after school. Louisa was drawing little triangles on a pad of paper. Jennie was staring hard at Brad.

"Well, it was your bright idea, Brad. You're the one who thought it would be so easy to work and get paid for it."

"Well, if it was such a dumb idea, how come you agreed to it?"

That kept Jennie quiet for a minute. "Listen," he told the girls. "More people need to know about our project. We can put more of Louisa's posters up, only this time we'll put them all over town, not just in the school." Brad liked the sound of it.

"You mean like in the windows of local stores?" Jennie asked.

"Sure. I bet everybody would let us put a poster in their windows. Louisa's horses are *so* pretty," Brad said. Louisa didn't look up, but Brad could tell she was smiling. She'd stopped drawing triangles and was now drawing little pictures of Partner.

"Great idea!" Jennie agreed. "We'll need at least another fifty posters. We can put them up on Friday and Saturday!"

"Well, you could put up the first two on Friday and Saturday," Louisa said, glancing up from her sketch. "I can only do about two a week," she explained.

"Brad, that was a rotten idea," Jennie said.

Silence hung in the air. The only sound was the gentle scratching of Louisa's pencils on her paper.

"We've got to find a way to get customers!" Jennie said.

Louisa picked up her black pencil and began coloring Partner's hoofs. "Why don't we go to our customers?" she asked. "You know, like a fund-raising thing?"

It was just the beginning of an idea, but it was enough. Suddenly Brad had it and he was really excited. It seemed to him that the answer was staring him in the face.

"A car wash!" he said. "We'll have a car wash. We can have it next Saturday and Sunday. We won't need to put up fancy signs, just simple ones that say CAR WASH. THIS WAY. You know, and then an arrow?"

Jennie and Louisa nodded. "Golly, if we charge two dollars per car, all we'd need is twenty-five cars and Partner's first month would be paid for." He didn't mention the price of the ad. "We can

use the teachers' parking lot at school —
there's a hose out there. Dad will sell us
some of the soap stuff and all we need
is old towels. We can have donuts and
coffee for our customers, too! It's a
snap!"

Brad's enthusiasm was contagious.
Jennie and Louisa agreed. Jennie even
told Brad it was the exact same thing
she was about to suggest. From Jennie,
that was high praise.

When the committee reported to the
whole class the next day, everybody was
excited about Brad's idea. Some people
would put up signs. Others were in
charge of towels and buckets. The school
gave them the coffee. The kids signed
up for times and jobs.

It seemed so simple.

Chapter 17

Washout

On Saturday morning, Brad practically jumped out of bed and into his clothes. It was The Big Day.

Within minutes, he was downstairs filling his bowl with cereal. He knew he'd need a good wholesome meal to carry him through the day, which would be very busy and filled with excitement. He drank his juice and refilled his glass. He ate two bowls of cereal and a banana. He was ready for anything. He thought.

"Oh, I'm so sorry," his mother said, coming into the kitchen.

"What are you sorry about?" Brad asked. "This is going to be a great day!"

His mother looked at him strangely —

as if she wondered what planet he'd come from.

"The weather, Brad. Did you look out the window?"

He did then. What he saw was a mean gray sky above a mist-covered world.

"That doesn't matter," Brad said. "We won't mind getting wet. After all, that's what car washes are for. What's a little sprinkle on us, compared to what Partner could have to suffer?"

"It's not really you kids I'm worried about," his mother said.

"I don't think grown-ups mind getting a little wet, either, do they, Mom?"

"Well, maybe," she said. But the "maybe" didn't sound very encouraging. That didn't matter, though, because Brad didn't hear her.

Brad got to the parking lot by 8:30. The car wash was scheduled to begin at 9:00. The class had decided that a lot of people liked to get their cars washed first thing in the morning, so they wanted to be ready.

And so they were.

By 9:30, there was still no sign of their first customer.

"I'm getting a donut," Zoe said.

"Get me one, too," Alison said.

"Hey, those are for the customers," Brad said.

"What customers?" Zoe asked him.

At ten o'clock, a car drove into the parking lot. It was Michael's mother bringing him there, late.

At 10:30, their first customer came in. It was Brad's mother. Since Brad — and everybody else — knew perfectly well that she could have her car washed for free at Brad's father's garage, everybody knew she'd come to the car wash just to be nice. So they did a nice job of washing. That was their first $2.

Then Alison's mother came in. Another $2 went into the box. Finally, Michael's mother came to get her car washed and to take Michael home. After

they left, both Alison and Brad stared expectantly at Zoe.

"Don't look at me," she said. "Our car is in the garage for repairs. One of you is going to have to give me a ride home."

They left at noon, turning over their towels to the next shift of Jennie, Jeremy, Rob, and Ellie. Brad would have liked a chance to see Jennie get splashed with the hose, but he suspected there wouldn't be much more hosing in the afternoon than there had been in the morning. The rain hadn't let up a bit.

He was right. By the end of the day, they had made $12, less the cost of the donuts and the soap for the wash. Their profit was $8.72. And that was the good news.

Sunday, it rained all day long. It wasn't a gentle sprinkle like Saturday. It was a drenching downpour. Brad stayed inside, staring at the rain and checking his arithmetic. The numbers didn't change. They still didn't have enough money to pay for *The Penny Saver* ad, much less Partner's first month at Akers Acres.

And he couldn't wait to hear what Jennie had to say about his bright idea at the next committee meeting.

Chapter 18

Jennie's Bright Idea

"I knew we shouldn't have done that!" Jennie said. She was walking back and forth in the library, where they were holding their committee meeting. "I knew it was a bad idea, but you were so sure it would be perfect. You were so sure we'd make a bundle with a car wash that you wouldn't even listen to me!"

Brad could hardly believe what he was hearing. Louisa was drawing circles around circles on her sketch pad. Each one was a little bigger than the last. Maybe it was a picture of Jennie's swelled head.

"Okay, Jennie. What's *your* idea?" Brad asked.

"Mine?" she said. She sounded surprised. "This is a committee. We're supposed to come up with ideas as a group. It's not just my job to have ideas."

Of course, that meant that Jennie didn't have any ideas. Louisa finished making the biggest circle and then she turned the paper over and started making squares. Maybe that was supposed to be a picture of Brad's head.

Jennie and Brad watched as Louisa filled in the paper. When she had drawn the largest possible square, she sighed.

"Something wrong?" Brad asked.

"I'm out of paper," she explained.

"Paper! That's it!" Jennie shrieked.

"What's 'it'?" Brad asked.

"We'll have a paper drive. You know how everybody just stacks up their old newspapers until there's a gigantic stack and then they don't know what to do with it?"

Brad supposed some people did stack up old newspapers, but not his family. His father always took the paper to the garage to do the crossword puzzle. Somehow, he couldn't imagine Jennie's family saving up old newspapers. What for? Double coupon day? Not likely.

"Okay, so there are a lot of newspapers stacked up. What do you want to do with them?"

"Sell them!" Jennie said. "There are lots of people who pay a lot of money for scrap paper. All we have to do is collect the paper and bring it in to them."

"How do we do it?" he asked.

"Well, first, we put up signs, and then we get somebody to drive for us, and we pick up the papers and sell them to a recycling place."

"Don't most people *give* papers to recycling places?"

"Not if they're trying to make money for a good cause, like saving the life of a poor old horse," Jennie said smartly.

Brad didn't understand why it was that if old newspapers were so valuable, everybody was forever trying to get rid of them. Brad began to tell Jennie how he thought her idea was weird, but she started talking louder.

"All right, Mr. Know-It-All. You're the one who got us into that awful car wash. And I can tell you that my clothes were absolutely ruined by the time I got home from it. If you think you're so smart, how come your idea was a disaster?"

Jennie was certainly right about that. So he decided to try hers. After all, if that didn't work, he could gloat the way she'd been gloating about the car wash, even though the rain wasn't at all his fault.

"Okay," he said. "We'll have a paper drive."

"This weekend," she said. "Then, we'll have the money we need to send Partner to Mr. Akers next week!"

"Oooooh," Louisa said.

Chapter 19

Jeremy's Leaves

"Why me?" Jeremy Gingrich asked. But there wasn't anybody there to answer. He was all alone. His only company was a rake and he wasn't happy about it.

When it came his turn to take a job for the class project, he was hoping he'd be able to walk a dog, or water plants for somebody going on vacation, or help paint a fence or something. He wanted to do something fun.

What did he get? He got a job raking leaves. Raking leaves was not fun. Definitely not fun.

Mrs. Atherton had this great big yard. All around the great big yard were great big trees. And on all the great big trees were great big leaves. She wanted some-body to rake up the yard and make the leaves into a neat pile that the garbage-men could collect. Looking at the mess in the yard, Jeremy figured it had been at least ten years since anybody had raked it.

Disgusted, he yanked away at the leaves, pulling them toward a very slow-growing pile.

"Say, Jeremy, what are you doing?" he heard someone yell.

Jeremy looked up. There was Billy Bruno. Billy was Jeremy's neighbor. He was two years older than Jeremy and he was a bully. Jeremy didn't like to admit it, but Billy had beaten him up more than once, and he was the kind of kid who was always looking for an excuse to do it again. Billy's friend Choo Choo Barrett was with him. Billy liked to have an audience when he beat people up. Jeremy was sure he was in for trouble.

"I said, what are you doing?" Billy asked more insistently.

"Raking leaves," Jeremy told him, but he knew that wouldn't be enough of an answer for Billy.

"I can see that, Jeremy. *Why* are you raking leaves?"

Now Jeremy was in a pickle. If he told Billy he was raking leaves to save a horse's life, Billy would beat him up. If he didn't answer him at all, Billy would beat him up. That wasn't much of a choice. But then Jeremy had an idea — an inspiration, in fact. He remembered something his father had told him about Tom Sawyer — a boy in a book who rooked his friends into doing his work for him. Jeremy figured he had nothing to lose by trying something like that, too.

"I'm raking leaves because it's fun," he told Billy.

"That's your idea of fun?" Billy asked. Billy pointed to his ear with his finger and made circles around it to tell Choo Choo he thought Jeremy was crazy. Jeremy saw him do it. Billy knew Jeremy

saw him do it. It was sort of a challenge.

Jeremy ignored them. He grabbed a rakeful of leaves and dragged it toward the pile. Billy and Choo Choo watched. Jeremy whistled happily, pulling some more leaves toward the pile. Smiling to himself, he skipped toward the edge of the yard and began forming a bunch of leaves, which he happily brought over to the main pile. Billy and Choo Choo watched. Jeremy smiled happily. In fact, he'd never seemed so happy in his life.

"You know," he said to Billy. "I'm awfully glad I got Mrs. Atherton to agree to let me rake leaves before you guys came along. If she'd seen you guys first, she probably would have let you do the raking. Too bad there's only one rake, though."

"There is?" Billy said.

And that was when Jeremy knew he had him.

"Yeah, just one," he said as he continued working at the scattered leaves.

Billy watched quietly for a while.

Choo Choo stared, too. "We have a rake at home," Billy said. "I could go get it."

"Nah, I don't think so," Jeremy said. "Mrs. Atherton said *I* could do this raking. She didn't say *you* could."

"But it's a big yard," Billy said. "I could work over there." He pointed to the far corner. The leaves in *that* corner were going to have to be raked the farthest.

"Give me a break, Billy," Jeremy said.

"You give *me* a break, Jeremy," Billy said, his eyebrows arching. Jeremy knew he was trying to sound threatening. It was time to give in.

"Okay, listen, Billy, I don't want any trouble from you. If you guys want to get your own rakes, I'd be glad to share. I don't suppose Mrs. Atherton will mind."

Billy and Choo Choo disappeared down the street. While they were gone, Jeremy carefully outlined an area for himself by raking a line across the yard. It was a very small section. That way, Billy would think he'd frightened Jeremy into letting him have the most.

When Billy and Choo Choo reappeared with their rakes a few minutes later, Jeremy told them to leave his section alone. They did. Quickly, the bigger boys set to work, whistling and smiling as Jeremy had been doing. They were having a wonderful time, but not as good a time as Jeremy had while he was raking his very small section of the great big yard.

And when the job was finally done, Billy and Choo Choo left Jeremy alone. They were going to see if they could find another yard to rake all by themselves, without Jeremy in their way.

That was okay with Jeremy. He knocked on Mrs. Atherton's door and collected the money from her.

Jeremy walked home whistling to himself. He knew that he'd beaten up Billy Bruno without ever laying a hand on him.

Chapter 20

Getting a Bundle

"Say, Dad," Brad said at breakfast.

His father lowered the newspaper and raised his eyebrows. "Yes, son?"

"Can I have the paper when you're done with it?"

"Sure," he agreed. "Want to read the sports section?"

"Not really. I just want to make sure we keep the paper for the paper drive."

"No problem, Brad," his father said. But when he left for work that day, he took the paper with him.

Brad strongly suspected that exactly the same scene had been repeated in the homes of everyone in his class that morning. It wasn't that the parents didn't *want* their children to have the newspapers. It was just that they were accustomed to doing something else with them — like throwing them away.

His mother saw his glum face when he realized what had happened to the paper, sports section and all.

"He's just not used to leaving the paper at home, Brad," she said, trying to comfort him. It wasn't very comforting.

"Well, we just saw perfectly good money walk out the door."

"But not a lot of money," Mrs. Carter said.

"Even a little money is perfectly good money," Brad told her.

"Say, Brad, if you want to make good money, I've got an idea," she said.

"What?" he asked suspiciously.

"Mr. Costello — "

"That old grump?" Brad said, interrupting his mother.

"Well, he's got some perfectly good money," she said. Mr. Costello was the

Carters' neighbor. He lived alone in the house next to theirs. He was an old man and he never had a nice word to say to anybody who had to chase a ball into his yard. The lady in the house on the other side of the Carters always liked to give Brad and his friends treats. Mr. Costello only gave them trouble.

"What could I do for him that would earn some perfectly good money?" Brad asked.

"He just needs help around the house," Mrs. Carter said. Brad could imagine what that meant. The house was a big old one, sort of spooky. He figured Mr. Costello might want someone to dust his skeleton collection or put oil on the torture machines in the basement/dungeon. Or to feed his pet tarantulas. Sure, working for him would be a barrel of laughs — all for perfectly good money.

"I'll think about it," Brad said. But he didn't mean it.

At school, Jennie spent a lot of time

reminding the class about the upcoming paper drive. Not that anybody could forget it, but since it was Jennie's idea, she took the opportunity to talk about it a lot. She also liked to remind the class — particularly Brad — that her father had volunteered to do the driving, so all they needed was a schedule of kids to be in the car with him.

They would start at two o'clock on Saturday afternoon. Jennie figured the car would be able to make a few trips to the recycling plant before dark. She assured the class that Rent a Third Grader would really get a bundle.

And that's exactly what they did get.

The first sign that something was going wrong came at 2:05, right after Jennie and her father picked Brad up at his house. As they were driving along the first street where they would collect papers, they saw a truck — a very large one — the kind that farmers used to carry cattle in. Only it didn't have cattle in it. It had newspapers in it.

"What's that?" Brad asked.

"Oh, probably nothing," Jennie said.

"That wasn't nothing. That was news-papers," Brad informed her.

Then another truck whizzed past them, also very large, also full of news-papers.

"And there's another one," Brad said. Jennie couldn't ignore it.

"Boy, it'll be a busy afternoon at the recycling center," Jennie said.

Mr. Everett stopped the car at the first house on the street. Brad and Jennie jumped out and rang the bell to ask for newspapers.

"But I already gave you all the ones I had," the woman said.

"No you didn't," Jennie contradicted her. "We just started. We haven't gotten any papers at all."

"Well, you won't get any here," the woman informed her.

And it was the same everywhere. It didn't take long to figure out what had happened. The third graders' paper drive had taken place right after the 4-H Club paper drive, and the town was cleaned out. The 4-H'ers had done a very thorough job.

After a fruitless hour driving through town in search of overlooked newspapers, Mr. Everett pulled into Brad's father's garage to buy some gas. As soon as Mr. Carter saw Brad and Jennie in the car, he came running out of his office, carrying a bundle of papers — all the ones he'd been saving since Brad had first started talking about the paper drive.

No matter how disappointed Brad was about the total failure of the paper drive, he was proud of his father, and they accepted the papers gladly. In fact, those were the only papers they got all afternoon. Even Jennie's mother had given her papers to the 4-H kids. Later, when they took Brad's father's newspapers to the recycling plant, the man there weighed the small bundle and gave Brad the money.

Twenty-five cents.

Brad gave the money to Mr. Everett to help pay for his gas. Mr. Everett had better manners than Jennie. He accepted the money.

Chapter 21

Zoe's Baby-sitting Service

"Hey, Mom, guess what?" Zoe asked her mother excitedly on Tuesday afternoon.

Her mother looked up from her computer screen. "Did you say something, dear?" she asked.

"Yes, guess what?" Zoe repeated.

"I couldn't," her mother said.

"I got a job. Remember I told you about Rent a Third Grader?"

Zoe's mother wrinkled her forehead. "Yes, yes, I remember now," she said. Zoe's mother sometimes didn't remember things. Zoe knew that asking her to remember something that happened that morning was something like asking an eighty-year-old what had happened on her fifth birthday. It wasn't that Zoe's mother was dumb or didn't care. It was because her own work used so much concentration that sometimes she didn't have much left for anybody else. "Hey, that's great!" she said, now pleased for Zoe. "What kind of job is it?"

"I really don't know yet, Mom. I'm supposed to call this lady. She just left a message at the school."

"Okay, so call her," her mother urged her.

Zoe looked uncomfortably at the phone.

"Are you shy about it?" her mother asked. Zoe nodded. "Want me to call while you get yourself a snack?" Zoe hated talking to strangers on the phone, and her mother knew that.

"Thanks, Mom."

Mrs. Chessman was not one to delay on anything. Once her mind was focused, there was no stopping her. Before Zoe had gotten the milk out of the refrigerator, her mother had the phone to her ear and was jotting down date and time. Before the cookies were out of the cabinet, her mother was hanging up.

"She wants you to baby-sit for her baby, Chris," Mrs. Chessman told Zoe. "Tomorrow afternoon I have to get you there by three-thirty on the dot. That's what Mrs. Carmen said. She needs you until about six-thirty. She pays two-fifty an hour." Mrs. Chessman handed Zoe the note with the Carmens' address and then she returned to her computer.

"Baby-sitting?" Zoe said. "Wow!" But her mother didn't hear her.

All of the next day at school, Zoe was too excited about her job to think. When Miss Bilgore asked her what seven times seven was, Zoe told her it was 3:30 to 6:30. A lot of the kids laughed. When the science teacher asked her why the dinosaurs disappeared from the earth, she told him it was because of changing diapers. When the gym teacher asked the class what game they wanted to play, Zoe just said, "Baby-sitting." Nothing this exciting had ever happened to her before.

By three o'clock, she'd decided she wanted to take little Chris for a walk. She *really* wanted to take the baby over to her friend Alison's house, but it was probably too far away and a baby-sitter couldn't take chances like crossing streets. Maybe she would spend the entire time holding Chris and giving the baby bottles. Maybe Chris would go to sleep in her arms. She sighed deeply, thinking how nice that would be.

When school was over at 3:15, her mother was waiting for her. Zoe practically flew out of the front door of the school to the car. After she'd buckled herself in, she remembered she had left her Red Reader in her desk. She flew back to her classroom and then flew back out to the car. Out of breath and puffing, she buckled herself in again and said, "Let's go." The one thing in the whole world that she didn't want to happen was to be late for her baby-sitting job.

It didn't take long to find the Carmens' house. It was exactly 3:30 when they got there. Mrs. Carmen was obviously in a hurry. As soon as she saw the Chessmans' car, she got into her own car, started the engine, and began backing out of the driveway. She waved at Zoe's mom, yelled "See you at six-thirty," and was gone.

"I'll be here then to pick you up, dear," Zoe's mother said. "And good luck."

Zoe unbuckled her seat belt and climbed out of the car. "Thanks, Mom," she said before she slammed the door. Her mother drove off. That was when Zoe began to wonder about a woman who would leave her baby alone in the house, even for a few minutes, when a baby-sitter arrived. How would she know where the bottles were? The diapers? The carriage? For that matter, how could she be sure whether Chris was a boy or a girl?

Determined to protect the baby, whatever kind it was, she marched right up to the front door of the house and went in.

It was a large house with a big front porch. On the left as she came in there was a dining room. To her right was a living room. Straight ahead was the kitchen and a wide flight of stairs. There was no sign of the baby on the first floor. Quietly, so as not to wake the baby, Zoe climbed the stairs. At the landing on the second floor, Zoe saw five doors and another flight of stairs. One by one, she opened the doors. Three bedrooms, linen closet, bathroom. No baby's room. No baby. Zoe was beginning to panic. Where *had* Mrs. Carmen hidden little Chris?

She went up the next flight of stairs. Now she could hear some noise. But it wasn't a baby sleeping. It was the noise of a television set. Three doors were at the top of those stairs. The first door was another bathroom. The next door was an attic. Very quietly, Zoe opened the third door, where the television sound was coming from. No baby, but there was a kid, a boy, watching a movie on a VCR.

"Hello?" Zoe said.

"Hi," said the boy. "Who are you?"

"I'm Zoe," she told him. "I'm the baby-sitter. Where's the baby?"

"There isn't any baby," he said.

"Am I in the wrong house?" Zoe asked, suddenly horrified. "Isn't this the Carmen house?"

"Yep," the boy said.

"Then, where's Chris? I'm supposed to take care of the baby," she insisted.

"*I'm* Chris," the boy said, standing up to switch off the television set. When he turned around, Zoe got a good look at him. He was at least twelve years old!

"*You're* Chris?"

"That's what I said, didn't I?" he asked, though he said it quite nicely. "As a matter of fact, I've been Chris for twelve and a half years — a lot longer than you've been Zoe, I'd guess," he said, smiling.

"How am I supposed to baby-sit for *you*?" she asked.

"Want to play Monopoly?" he asked, in answer.

Zoe shrugged. "Sure," she said. "You play Free Parking?"

"Of course," he said.

Chris led her back down to the living room, where he got out the Monopoly game. As he set it up, he explained the situation.

"See, my mother thinks I need a baby-sitter, even though I'm in the seventh grade and *nobody* in the seventh grade needs a baby-sitter, unless their folks are going to be out really late at night. Anyway, she keeps getting sitters for me. I wish she'd stop. I don't need a sitter. I'm okay by myself. Somebody's always home at our neighbors', and my grandma lives just a few blocks away. I can take care of myself. But my mother keeps getting me sitters. At this rate, I'll have to have a baby-sitter to take me to the prom the night before graduation!"

"Gosh, I stay by myself in the afternoons," Zoe said.

"See what I mean?" Chris said. "And how old are you?"

"Eight," Zoe said. "And a half," she added.

"I'll take the shoe. What do you want to be?"

"The racing car," she said.

They played Monopoly. Zoe won. Then they had a snack. Zoe said they shouldn't eat too much so they wouldn't ruin their appetites for dinner. It was the sort of thing baby-sitters said to her, so she thought she was doing her job. Chris laughed and she laughed, too, because it was funny. They each ate only three cookies. Then they each got their homework books and were doing their reading assignments when Mrs. Carmen came back.

"Who are *you?*" she demanded when she saw Zoe.

"I'm Zoe Chessman, the baby-sitter," Zoe told her with a straight face.

At first, Mrs. Carmen just stared. It was as if she couldn't think of anything to say. Then she glanced at Chris and back at Zoe. For a second, Zoe was afraid she was going to blow up, and she did — in a way. The next sound was a sort of explosion. It was a snort as Mrs. Carmen started laughing. Chris began laughing along with her and the next thing Zoe knew, she was giggling as well.

"You mean I hired *you* to baby-sit for Chris?"

Zoe nodded in answer, since she was laughing too hard.

"It's okay, Mom," Chris said. "She didn't get into any trouble. And she wouldn't let me have more than three cookies."

"Oh, Chris, Chris," Mrs. Carmen said finally, when she wasn't laughing anymore. "You've been telling me you were too old for a sitter. Is that why you gave me this phone number at the school?"

"Yes, Mom," he said.

Then Zoe understood. She'd been set

up by Chris to convince his mother she could leave him alone — at least in the afternoon.

"Okay, Chris. I get the point. I guess I've been going a bit overboard, haven't I?"

"Yeah," he said. But he said it nicely. When Zoe first realized that Chris had been using her, she was ready to be angry, but he was so nice about it, and it was working, that she really couldn't blame him. After all, it *was* funny.

"Okay, I guess I owe you some money, Zoe, right?" Mrs. Carmen said.

"Maybe you ought to give it to Chris," Zoe offered.

"No way," he said. "You're the one who wouldn't let me have the cookies!"

"Okay," Zoe agreed. "I'll take it."

Mrs. Carmen carefully counted out the $7.50 and gave it to Zoe. Zoe thanked Mrs. Carmen and stuffed the money in her pocket. Just then, her own mother honked.

"Gotta go," Zoe said. Chris and his

mother said good-bye. Zoe skipped down the stairs and down the front walk to her mother's car.

"Was it a cute baby?" her mother asked as they drove home.

Zoe thought about Chris' nice smile and his polite way. She thought about what a good sport he was about losing the Monopoly game to her and how he teased her when she'd let him have only three cookies.

"Yes," she said. "He *was* kind of cute."

Chapter 22

Facing Facts

Brad didn't have the heart to tease Jennie about the paper drive's failure. In fact, he felt a little sorry for her. Sure, she could be a bratty know-it-all, but she cared about Partner and she had worked very hard. She'd worked as hard as he and Louisa had. They were all giving it their best and it wasn't working — unless he counted the $4.25 Melissa Jefferson had earned.

Even that had been a near disaster. Brad forgot that the money was in his pocket when he put his pants in the wash. The dollar bills came out a little fuzzy, but they were still dollar bills. The quarter got really shiny, though.

The clean money went into the box with the money from the car wash and the few dollars Ellie, Jeremy, and Zoe had earned. All together, the Treasurer counted $23.97. No matter how he counted it, one thing was clear: It wasn't enough.

Of course, he had to tell Jennie and Louisa about how little money they had and about how much they owed — especially to *The Penny Saver*. They were horrified. Louisa was stunned to silence, as usual. Jennie seemed to be feeling the same way Brad was because she said it was too bad the paper drive hadn't earned as much as the car wash. It was true, of course, but it wasn't like Jennie to realize it.

Brad couldn't stand the idea that his brainchild, Rent a Third Grader, was going to fail. When he saw Mr. Snodgrass' van parked in front of the Police Station later that day, he knew it was time for desperate action. On his way home from school, he made the decision.

Instead of going directly home, he rang Mr. Costello's doorbell.

There was a very long wait before there was any answer. Brad stood awkwardly on the porch, glancing in through the windows, nearly opaque with dirt. His heart was beating so loudly, he was sure he could hear it. He hoped nobody was home. He hoped Mr. Costello was away for a long time.

Just as he was about to retreat down the stairs, a light flicked on in the hallway. A few seconds later, the door opened a crack.

"Who is it?" the gruff voice demanded.

Brad felt ill with fear.

"It's me, Brad Carter, sir," he managed to say. He gulped. "My mother said you might want to hire me to help you around the house or something, Mr. Costello. See, my class and me, we're trying to earn money for a good cause, you see it's the police horse and we want to save him but it's going to take a lot of money and we want to earn it so I was wondering if I could do something for you that would earn me some money, sir?"

No doubt about it, that was the strangest sentence Brad had ever uttered, but Mr. Costello seemed to understand.

"Come Monday at four," he said. "I'll pay you a dollar an hour if you're any good."

"Yes, sir," Brad said, turning to leave.

"And here," Mr. Costello said, extending his arm through the crack in the door. In his hand was a baseball. It was the baseball Brad had thrown into Mr. Costello's fenced-in yard two weeks earlier. He'd been too scared to go ask for it then. "This is yours, right?" the old man asked.

"Yes, uh, thank you, sir, Mr. Costello," Brad said, taking the baseball from the man's hand.

"Got to learn to throw better," Mr. Costello said. "More wrist, less elbow.

You get more control that way." The door closed.

It was a few minutes before Brad could move. He stood in front of Mr. Costello's door, holding the baseball in front of him, staring at it.

Chapter 23

———◆———

Brad and Partner

The next Saturday was an important day. It was the day of the Police Department retirement party for Officer Chambliss. Thanks to Miss Bilgore's class, Partner was there, too.

Miss Bilgore's class was invited to the party, and so was everybody else in town.

The Mayor gave a speech. Chief Mallory gave a speech. The retired Chief of Police gave a speech. The retired Mayor gave a speech.

It was very boring for everybody — except Officer Chambliss. Brad turned around in his seat to look at the crowd. Theirs was a pretty small town. He knew most of the people there. But there was one person there he wished he didn't know at all. For just six rows behind his class was Mr. Mustache himself, Rodney Snodgrass. Brad shivered. He could have sworn that old Snodgrass wasn't looking at Officer Chambliss. He was glaring at Partner.

While the speeches droned on, Brad got a mental picture of himself and his classmates forming a human chain to prevent Snodgrass from rushing up and grabbing Partner. He was glad they were sitting in front of the man. They would protect the horse!

Brad was sitting between Jennie and Louisa. Jennie noticed that he wasn't paying any attention to the speeches, so she nudged him. He turned around and faced forward again. That way, he could watch Partner carefully. Officer Chambliss had groomed him like never before. Partner's coat was so shiny that the bright sun gleamed off it. (In fact, the sun was so bright that Brad knew it would have been a great day for a car wash.) Partner's mane had been combed and trimmed and lay smoothly on his neck. His tail was neatly braided with yellow and blue ribbons — the official colors of the town Police Department. His saddle and bridle had been polished and buffed, too. He looked swell.

Brad shifted again in his folding chair. It squeaked. Jennie and Louisa both looked at him. Their chairs squeaked, too. They all smiled a little, then looked ahead.

Brad heard somebody behind him clear his throat. He was certain it was old Snodgrass. Then he looked at Partner standing patiently near the podium. The horse blinked. Then he blinked again. Brad could have sworn he was winking at him. And then, right then, Brad realized that no matter how the whole thing had begun, that wasn't what it was about now. It wasn't about social studies or garages. It wasn't about having the class, or the police, think he was wonderful. It wasn't even about Jennie or Louisa. It was about Partner.

Brad looked at the shiny clean horse and really understood, for the first time. No matter how he'd gotten into this, the only thing he cared about now was saving Partner. He absolutely couldn't bear the thought of that beautiful horse going to the HappiPet Food Company.

Just then, Brad heard his name, sort of. Officer Chambliss was speaking.

" . . . so when Burt, Jane, and Lucy and the rest of Miss Billman's class volunteered to earn the money for Partner's retirement . . . " (Brad wasn't surprised that Office Chambliss, who couldn't remember anybody's name, never made a mistake on Partner's name) " . . . well, I just knew I could rely on them, and that my Partner can, too." Everybody started clapping and the class had to stand up. When they turned around, Brad noticed that old Snodgrass' seat was empty. He was glad.

But still, things weren't looking good. More than half their time had been used up and they didn't have enough money to pay for a *week*, much less a month.

The Police Department's dog, Nero, ran through the party. Dogs made Brad think of dog food. Brad couldn't bear to look at Nero.

Chapter 24

One Step Forward — Two Steps Back

After school on Monday, Brad went straight to Mr. Costello's for two of the oddest hours he'd ever spent.

Inside Mr. Costello's house it was dark and dusty, just the way it looked from the outside. All except the glassed-in porch in the back. That was like a greenhouse. There was wicker furniture on it — tables, chairs, loungers. But mostly, there were plants on it. There were hundreds of plants on it. Little ones, medium-sized ones, and big ones. Some of them were almost trees.

"Boy, you've got some kind of green thumb, huh?" he said, but then he was sorry right away because it seemed like such a dumb thing to say. Mr. Costello didn't seem to notice at all.

"I'd like you to water these now," he told Brad. He showed Brad where the hose was and explained how to use the nozzle so he could go from pot to pot and water the plants without watering the floor.

"You understand what I want you to do?" Mr. Costello asked sternly.

Brad nodded. It seemed simple to Brad. He didn't understand why Mr. Costello needed his help.

Mr. Costello sat in one of the loungers and watched, silently, while Brad went from plant to plant. "Not too much on that one," he told Brad. Brad sprinkled it gently.

"This one looks really dry, Mr. Costello," Brad said.

Mr. Costello grunted. Brad put a lot of water on it. Mr. Costello didn't say anything. Brad thought that meant he'd done the right thing. Since Mr. Costello was watching every move Brad was making, he was certain he'd be told if he made a mistake. Brad felt like he was taking a test.

Some of the plants hung from beams in the ceiling. Brad had to climb on a ladder to reach them. Mr. Costello could have reached most of them easily without a ladder.

When Brad finished the last plant, Mr. Costello stood up and walked around to each pot, inspecting Brad's work. He grunted again.

"Okay, Brad. You did all right. Here's your pay. Come back Friday. Same time."

Brad nodded and took the money from Mr. Costello. He ran to the door and ran all the way home. It wasn't until he was standing in his own kitchen that he looked at the money Mr. Costello had given him for two hours of watering plants.

It was five dollars!

On Tuesday and Wednesday, Brad tried to have another committee meeting. He wanted to tell Jennie and Louisa about the five dollars and he wanted to see if they had any other ideas about how to make money. Jennie and Brad thought Wednesday afternoon would be fine, but Louisa didn't agree.

"I'm much too busy. Too busy," she told them. "Aren't you?"

"Well, sure we're busy," Brad said.

"Okay, then afterwards," Louisa said.

"After what?" Brad asked.

"Thursday, of course," Louisa said and then dashed off, trailing colored pencils behind her. Even when she came back to pick them up, Brad couldn't get any more information out of her.

Until Thursday. On Thursday morning, Brad saw Louisa arrive at school. Her mother drove her because she was trying to carry so much. She had three cartons. Brad couldn't believe it. He shook his head and walked off, not even curious about what was in the cartons.

He didn't see Louisa again until later that morning. It turned out she'd gotten special permission to miss Class Meeting and the first part of Arithmetic. He wondered what she was up to.

He found out soon enough. The minute Arithmetic was over, Louisa rushed over to him.

"Okay, now you and Jennie can sell your cookies!" she said excitedly.

Brad looked for Jennie in the rush of classmates. When she saw the look on his face, she came running over. "What's up?" she asked.

"You can put out all the cookies now," Louisa told Jennie.

Jennie and Brad exchanged looks. "What cookies?" Brad asked.

"For the cookie sale, of course," Louisa said.

"What cookie sale?" Jennie asked.

So far, this conversation wasn't going anywhere and Brad was getting a bad feeling about it.

"The Rent a Third Grader Cookie Sale, Brad," she said. "*That's* what cookie sale!"

"I hate to say this, Louisa, but what

Rent a Third Grader Cookie Sale?"

"Oh," Louisa said vaguely. "I guess I forgot to tell you about it, huh?" she said.

Brad and Jennie nodded. Together with Louisa they walked out of the classroom. The class was going to Science now. As soon as they got into the hall, Brad and everybody else saw the work Louisa had done. The entire hallway was decorated with crepe paper and streamers. There were balloons, all painted to look like they had chocolate chips in them. There were posters every few feet announcing the cookie sale. Louisa had drawn positively delicious-looking cookies on them.

Then all three of the committee co-chairpeople were surrounded by classmates asking about the cookie sale. It was hopeless. Louisa was about to burst into tears and their classmates were going to be angry when they found out there *wasn't* any cookie sale.

"Jennie," Brad said. "You take Louisa back into the classroom." Jennie put an arm on Louisa's shoulder and led her back to their empty homeroom. She'd be able to cry there without anybody making fun of her. Brad took care of the hungry third graders. He explained that there had been a mistake and the bell was about to ring for Science. They shuffled off.

Brad went into Room 209-3 and found Jennie handing Louisa tissues. Louisa was a regular tear machine. But Brad couldn't believe how much work she had done. And it wasn't going to do them, or Partner, any good. At first, he thought he ought to scream at her. Nobody in the world should be allowed to be that forgetful.

"Say, Brad," she said, between sniffles. "I've got an idea. Why don't we have the cookie sale *next* Thursday? We could leave the signs up until then."

Brad could just picture how the crepe paper would droop, waiting for the cookie sale. He knew some of the kids would write all over Louisa's beautiful posters. The balloons would shrivel.

"We sure would have given everybody enough warning," Louisa said hopefully.

He just knew they would all be laughed at and *that* wouldn't help Partner, either. Brad shook his head gently.

"Brad's right," Jennie said. "It was a good idea, though. I'm really sorry it didn't work."

"Me, too," Brad added.

Louisa knew they were right. She blew her nose a final time and then the three of them went into the hallway, where they began removing the decorations. The balloons and the crepe paper made a very sad pile on the floor.

The co-chairpeople were very late for Science. Nobody asked them why.

Chapter 25

Mr. Costello's Collection

"Brad, dear," his mother greeted him. "There's a letter for you on the hall table."

Brad didn't even bother to hope it was a letter about the Big Prize Jackpot, making him their first million-dollar winner (he always entered contests whenever he could). He knew what it was. It was the bill from *The Penny Saver*. He went to his cigar-box treasury. At least he had enough money to pay that bill.

He gave his mother the cash and she wrote a check for the ads. He addressed the envelope and put it in the mailbox, to be picked up the next morning. At least something had gone right, but it hardly made up for everything that had gone wrong.

On Friday after school, Brad went back to Mr. Costello's. He was expecting to water the plants again and he hoped he'd get another five dollars, too. After all, the first payment to Mr. Akers was due this week.

When Mr. Costello opened the door, he led Brad right back to the plant room, but instead of giving him a hose, he gave him a great big dusty box and sat him down at the large glass-topped table.

"Here, son," Mr. Costello said, removing the top from the dusty carton. "You did a good job with the plants. Now, this is what I *really* need you for."

Brad had been right. The plants *were* a test. But for what? He stared at the carton. All he could see were old cards of some kind.

"That's my collection," Mr. Costello told him.

Brad looked carefully. There, in front

of him, was an entire carton full of baseball cards. Not today's baseball cards. These were baseball cards from the 1920s and 1930s. They were for some of the most famous — and least famous — players of all time: Ty Cobb in 1923, the year he hit .340 for Detroit. There was a card for Dizzy Dean in 1934, the year he had a 30–7 record for St. Louis. Then there was Cy Perkins, who played for the Philadelphia Athletics. Good and bad were all mixed in and, as far as Brad was concerned, they were all wonderful.

"Are these real?" he asked.

"Yes, they are," Mr. Costello told him. "I chewed all the bubble gum myself, too."

Brad laughed and then was surprised to find himself laughing. The last thing he ever expected to do with Mr. Costello was to laugh. Mr. Costello laughed as well.

"Well, what am I supposed to do with them?" Brad asked.

"I've been saving these things for

years, Brad," he said. "I always knew that one day they'd be valuable and I think that day is now. I hate to part with them, but I need the money and I'm going to have to sell them. Before I do, I need to store them properly and catalogue them. I want you to help me."

"You *have* to sell them?"

"Yes, I do. My daughter — well, it's just time for me to sell 'em."

"And you're going to pay me to look at old baseball cards?" Brad asked. He could hardly believe his good luck.

"Yes, I am. I can't see so well, and I've got to get this done soon. If a dollar an hour isn't enough, would you take two?"

Brad was embarrassed that Mr. Costello had misunderstood him.

"Oh, no, sir. No, it's not that at all. I mean, if I could, I'd probably pay *you* just to be able to look at them. These guys are the greatest — and to see their *real* cards, not the modern ones. I think I'm pretty lucky, that's all."

"Okay, then, two dollars an hour. And I'll show you how to throw a ball."

"Did you play baseball?" Brad asked.

"Not me. Though I wished I could have. My dad was an outfielder in the National League a long time ago. Not a very good one. But he taught me to love the sport. And he taught me to throw properly."

And then they began their work. They had to count all the cards, and then pile them by year and then by club. Mr. Costello let Brad take as long as he needed to look at as many of them as he wanted. Brad hardly ever knew two hours to go by so quickly.

Chapter 26

————•————

A Temporary Solution

The next afternoon, Brad sat on the bed in his room and made a list of things he didn't want to think about:
1. *HappiPet Food Company*
 He didn't actually believe Mr. Snodgrass was riding around town with his van trying to find an opportunity to snatch Partner. It just seemed that way.
2. *The bill from Akers Acres that's about to come in the mail*
3. *The cookie sale*
4. *The paper drive*
 He knew it wasn't true that either Louisa or Jennie had meant to have her plan fail. But at least when the car wash

was a disaster, it wasn't his fault. He hadn't made the rain fall from the sky.

5. *The car wash*

There. He'd admitted it. He couldn't even stand to think about his own crummy plan.

6. *Dogs*

It was true. He'd gotten to the point where he was beginning to resent dogs who might, just *might,* some time in their lives eat dog food that contained horse meat.

7. *Eighteen dollars and seventy-six cents*

That was the amount of money he *didn't* have to pay the Akers Acres bill.

Brad looked at the list. He crumpled it up and threw it across the room toward the wastebasket. It missed, but he didn't care. He didn't even want to think about the list.

There was a knock at his door.

"Come in," he said.

His mother opened the door. "Brad, dear," she began. He knew that she knew that he didn't want to hear what she was going to say. She always called him "Brad, dear" when she had to break some bad news to him.

"Yeah?"

"You had a letter today. It's from Akers Acres." She had the envelope in her hand.

It was more than Brad could stand. He knew that would be the bill and he knew he couldn't pay it yet. But he *had* to or Snodgrass would snatch Partner. His eyes brimmed with tears. He wasn't a tear machine like Louisa, but he really couldn't help it. Before the first tear reached his cheek, his mother was sitting on his bed, hugging him.

"You know what I was thinking?" his mother said.

"What?" he snuffled.

"I was thinking we might work out some kind of temporary arrangement."

"For what?"

"Well, perhaps you'd like to arrange a loan?"

Brad sat up. "You mean like from

Jennie's dad's bank? He'd *give* us the money. I know he would, but that's not what I want to do."

"I know that, Brad. No. That's not what I mean. I mean a loan, just to tide you over so you can pay this bill. You've got some money in the cigar box, don't you?"

"Well, sure I do. You know that. You washed most of it when I left it in my pocket," he said. His mother laughed. That made him feel a little better.

"Yes, I did," she agreed. "If I recall, from my laundering operations, you need about twenty dollars to pay this bill."

"Eighteen dollars and seventy-six cents," Brad said.

"Well, your father and I will lend you that amount of money — to be paid back at the rate of two-fifty a week."

"That's how much I get in allowance," Brad said.

"So it is," Mrs. Carter said. "But this is a loan to your class project — not to you."

"Yeah, but if those guys don't make any money at all, then I can pay it back to you."

"I suppose so," his mother agreed.

"Deal," Brad said, offering his hand.

"Deal," his mother said, giving him a high five.

Chapter 27

Reunion with Partner

As soon as the Akers Acres bill was paid, Partner moved in. It was a wonderful day for Miss Bilgore's class. Louisa made a big picture of Rodney Snodgrass and pasted it to a bulletin board. She brought some darts to class, and the kids all practiced throwing them at their Snodgrass dart board. Miss Bilgore let them do it until Miss Mortimer came in to tell Miss Bilgore that they were making too much noise. They didn't mind stopping. Everybody had had a chance to throw the darts, and most of them had gone into old Snodgrass' nose. It made Brad feel better.

Then Miss Bilgore told the class she'd

arranged another trip to the farm. This time, of course, Partner would be there, running around in the field that had been empty before, playing with the horses who already lived there, eating the sweet grass that already grew there.

When the day came, everybody in the class brought an apple or some carrots or a sugar lump for Partner. They sang "The Last Round-Up" for the entire trip on the bus. Miss Bilgore sat in the front with Zoe because she usually got sick on bus trips. She didn't get sick this time. The ride went quickly.

When they arrived at the farm, all twenty-seven children from Miss Bilgore's class climbed onto the rail fence around Partner's pasture, even though Mr. Akers said it wasn't a good idea. Two children fell off the fence onto the muddy ground. One got a splinter in her hand. Another got a splinter where he sat. None of them cared. They were all too happy to see Partner.

At first, Partner was at the far end

of the pasture, munching happily on grass. But the wind must have carried the smell of the apples, carrots, and sugar to him, for he soon came cantering over to the children, greeting his old friends, eating the goodies they'd brought him. After he'd had five snacks, Mr. Akers gathered the rest and said he'd give them to Partner over the next couple of days. It wasn't a good idea to give him too many snacks at once, Mr. Akers said.

Zoe Chessman, who no longer looked green, as she had on the bus, brought out her camera. "Okay, I want to get a picture of everyone in the class and Partner," she announced. "Stand in his pasture in front of the old apple tree."

It took them a long time to get into a group that Zoe could photograph all at once. Jennie spent a lot of that time making sure she would be in the front row in the center. In the end, Miss Bilgore put Brad there, with Louisa on one side and Jennie on the other.

Mr. Akers held Partner at the back of the group. Miss Bilgore stood on the other side of the horse. Mrs. Akers agreed to take the picture so that even Zoe would be in it. Everybody smiled. Mrs. Akers took four pictures to be sure at least one would come out.

Then, while the class ate their picnic lunches, Mr. Akers put a saddle on Partner and said that the boys and girls could each have their picture taken sitting on Partner — if Zoe had enough film. Zoe had enough film. The only difficult part was getting Louisa to come down off Partner once she was on him. She really loved that horse. Brad smiled to see how happy she was, sitting on him.

When they finished taking pictures, the children began to play around the farm, enjoying the sunny, warm day and the fresh country air. Louisa climbed back into the saddle and sat there happily.

Brad, Jeremy, and Rob went over to

the pigsty. There, instead of just one very fat sow, was a very fat sow and twelve piglets. They were smelly, but they were awfully cute. While the boys watched, the little pigs played together, almost like kittens. They were just a little bigger than kittens, too. The sow, Mildred, was sleeping soundly in the afternoon sunshine.

Rob climbed over the fence into the pigsty. His feet sank into the muck. When he tried to walk, his shoes stuck in the mud, coming out with a sticky, bubbly, gucky sound at each step. It was irresistible. Jeremy climbed in, too. He got a splinter in his finger on the way over the fence.

"Say, Jeremy, do you think you could catch one of these piglets?" Rob asked. It was a dare.

"Sure," Jeremy said, gucking his way across the mud that separated him from the piglets. Jeremy would do *anything* on a dare.

The piglets scattered quickly. They

didn't weigh very much, and they had teeny little feet that slid right into the mud and right out of it with every step.

"One's coming this way!" Rob yelled. "I'll get him!"

The piglet apparently realized that Rob was going to grab for it and dodged to the right. Rob shifted in that direction, too — faster than his shoes could shift in the mud. His left foot came out of the mud. His left shoe didn't. Neither his right foot nor his right shoe moved at all. Rob fell into the mud.

Rob was a total mess. Jeremy started laughing. Brad, watching from the other side of the fence, did, too. Until he saw that the ruckus had awakened Mildred and she was standing up to get a better view of the situation. She snorted. He could tell right away that she didn't like having strangers messing around with her piglets. Then, in spite of her huge bulk, she began running toward Rob.

Rob was too scared to move.

"Jeremy!" yelled Brad. "Get Rob out of there!"

Jeremy saw the danger and started walking toward Rob. But he was slow. Very slow.

Brad couldn't stand it anymore. He swung open the gate to the pen and stepped in, as carefully but as quickly as he could, hoping he'd be able to rescue Rob before Mildred got to him. Three slow, gucky steps and he reached out to Rob. Rob took Brad's hand and stood up.

Mildred was closing in on them. She seemed to be getting angrier with every step.

"Get her attention!" Brad yelled to Jeremy. Quickly, Jeremy started flapping his arms and quacking. Brad couldn't, for the life of him, figure out why Jeremy was quacking, but it worked. Mildred stopped in her tracks and began eyeing Jeremy. Jeremy was scared. He took the two steps remaining to the far side of the fence and leaped out of the pigsty and into the goat pen.

Mildred returned her attention to Rob and Brad. Jeremy had given them just enough time to guck their way back to the open gate. The boys nearly threw themselves out of the sty and, with a final effort, Brad slammed the gate closed two seconds before Mildred reached it.

But, unfortunately, it was two seconds *after* the last of the piglets escaped through the gate that Brad had left open.

"Oh, no!" he said, watching twelve little pink piglets squeal with joy as they skittered down the hill, under the rail fence, and into Partner's pasture.

Chapter 28

————— ◆ —————

Disaster!

Disaster.

There was no other word for it.

Zoe saw it first. She clicked her camera, photographing one of the piglets running free. She heard Brad, Jeremy, and Rob yelling like crazy.

"The piglets are out! Catch 'em!" Zoe called out.

The boys and girls scattered in the field, almost as quickly as the piglets had, but the piglets had an advantage. They were so little, they were hard to see in the sweet grass.

Louisa, however, could see almost everything. She was still in the saddle on Partner's back.

"There's one over there," she said, pointing to the right. Alison ran in that direction. "And one over on the far side of the apple tree." She pointed. Mark went to chase it down. Zoe climbed onto the rail fence, taking pictures of her classmates' unsuccessful efforts to catch the piglets. Jennie climbed up beside her.

"We've got to get up higher," she said to nobody in particular, but everybody knew she was right.

"The apple tree!" Louisa cried out.

"Good idea," Jennie said, jumping down from the fence and running toward the tree. She scaled the branches as quickly as she could. Within a few minutes, she was very near the top and had a complete view of the pasture.

"Brad!" Jennie called. "Get everyone together!"

He signaled to everybody, calling them to the apple tree. When they were all nearby, Jennie spoke to them from on high.

"Okay, here's the plan," she said. Brad hadn't known she had a plan, but for once, he was really glad she did. "I want you to make a big circle around the edge of the pasture. The idea here is to chase the piglets toward the center of a circle that will get smaller and smaller. Once you're in place, all begin walking toward this tree that is in the middle of the field. Don't try to catch any of the piglets right away. Just make them come together. We're going to form a human fence!"

"And what if some of them get outside the human fence?" Louisa asked from the saddle, where she sat.

"Well, that's what you're for," Jennie told her.

"Me?"

"Yes, you. You're on the horse. You're in charge of the round-up."

"Me?"

"Yes, *you*," Jennie told her. Brad thought that was inspired. After all, Louisa had showed dogged determination throughout the work of their committee. There was no way Louisa would give up now.

"Come on, Partner," Louisa said to the horse. "We've got a job to do."

Almost as if he understood, Partner turned and loped across the pasture. Louisa sat high in the saddle.

Chapter 29

The Last Round-Up

In a flash, the classmates formed a very large circle around the edge of the pasture, and therefore around all the piglets, they hoped. Everybody was in the circle except Jennie, who was in the apple tree; Louisa, who was on the horse; Zoe, who was everywhere, taking pictures; and Jessica, who had been assigned the job of keeping Miss Bilgore and Mr. and Mrs. Akers on the other side of the barn until the piglets were recaptured.

Brad, Jeremy, and Rob were in the center of the circle. They'd brought the four canvas bags Miss Bilgore had used to tote the picnic lunches (and which were now empty) to carry recaptured piglets to the pigsty.

From the squeals the piglets made, everyone could tell right away that the shrinking circle was working. As the boys and girls walked closer and closer to each other, they shooed the piglets toward the center of the circle. The piglets seemed to be intent on running. They didn't seem to care in which direction. They mostly ran where they were shooed.

But suddenly, one shot out from between Mark and Alison. Brad waved his arms to show Jennie what had happened. Jennie signaled to Louisa, who nudged Partner into action. It was as if Partner had spent his whole life rounding up piglets in pastures, and none of it standing by the crosswalk at the elementary school or leading the Founder's Day Parade. He knew just what to do.

Louisa clung to the saddle with both hands and let Partner do the work. He did it. First, he circled around the piglet and then stood still as a statue until the piglet came near. When he was within striking distance, Partner pretended to charge at the piglet. Louisa was nearly bounced off the horse, but the piglet got the message. It turned and ran in a beeline for the center of the children's circle.

"Got it!" Brad called out, holding the wriggling piglet. Just before the piglet scrambled out of his grasp, Brad tucked it into a sack. Right after that, Jeremy put a second one in a bag. He handed the bag to Rob, who carried it over to the pigsty and returned the piglets to Mildred's care. He ran back for another load.

From the top of the apple tree, Jennie spotted a stray who had escaped the circle unnoticed. She waved her arms to get Louisa's attention. Louisa and Partner followed her signals and found the piglet. It was trying to burrow into a cool place near a large rock in the pasture.

Louisa climbed down from Partner.

She bent down and picked up the piglet. She held it in her arms like a baby. It looked up at her. Louisa thought it smiled. It was warm and pink and sweet and she loved it right away. Very carefully, she balanced the piglet on Partner's withers while she climbed back into the saddle from the top of the rock. When she was back up, she picked up the piglet and cradled it in her left arm. Its eyes closed and it went to sleep, sighing deeply.

Across the field, Brad yelled, "Got another one!"

"Me, too!" Rob howled.

"Here's one," said Alison.

Jennie saw a pair of piglets heading back toward the edge of the circle. She yelled at Michael and Melissa, who were closest to them. As soon as they spotted the pair, they began shooing as loudly as they could to get the piglets to turn around and head back to the center. That didn't work, so they each dived for one of the piglets and somehow trapped them at the same time. ·

"Victory!" Michael yelled, trying to grasp the wiggling pink mass firmly. He smiled triumphantly.

"Here comes another!" Jennie called out from the tree. A third piglet was headed their way. They didn't want to let go of the piglets they were holding, but the running piglet seemed determined to escape. Suddenly, there was the sound of hoofbeats. Louisa and Partner had arrived! The thump of the horse's hoofs frightened the little runaway. It turned right around and ran directly into Rob's waiting arms — and bag.

"Bingo!" he yelled.

The kids cheered.

Then Jeremy bagged another one. That was ten.

There were no more in sight. Two were missing. The boys and girls put all the captured piglets back in the pigsty and began searching for the last two.

"Maybe there *were* only ten," Melissa suggested.

"Nope," Brad said definitely. "There were twelve. I counted them. For sure."

They returned to the pasture to search carefully. It didn't take long. Number eleven had found a little muddy place on the shady side of a rock and was scratching its back in the mud. Melissa Jefferson put it in a bag. Number twelve was sound asleep in a patch of pink wildflowers, which had camouflaged it. Ellie Vanquist carried it all the way back to the pigsty without awakening it.

"There," Jennie said, happily slamming the gate on the final piglet.

Brad felt happy, too. Sure, it had been a disaster, but it had worked out okay, and there was no doubt about it, it had been fun. In fact, it had been funny, too. He remembered how silly Michael had looked, watching helplessly as the piglet tried to escape the circle. He remembered watching Louisa balance the piglet on Partner's withers. It had looked silly. In fact, a lot of the whole adventure had looked silly.

Suddenly, Brad *had* to laugh. He sat down under the apple tree and began laughing helplessly. He'd been so worried for so long that the laughter made him feel wonderful. Nothing could go wrong, he decided, when he and his friends could manage to work together and catch a crazy bunch of wild piglets in a horse pasture on a sunny school day.

"I've got an idea!" he said.

"What?" Jennie asked.

"It's a new campaign for Rent a Third Grader. You don't just get one kid, you get a whole class — and we specialize in round-ups!"

It was a pretty silly idea, but one part of it wasn't silly. The serious part was the one about getting the whole class. What was really good — and what had really worked — was the fact that they'd been a team. One third grader was okay, but when the whole class worked together and cooperated, well, it seemed to Brad that they could do almost anything — even beat old Snodgrass!

Then Jennie started laughing. She sat down next to Brad. He began laughing as well, thinking about how funny they must have looked. And then Jeremy joined them. Jeremy's laugh was contagious. Within seconds, absolutely everybody was giggling, remembering the silly adventure they'd had. Even Louisa was laughing — and that made everybody feel even better.

Until Miss Bilgore and Mr. and Mrs. Akers appeared with Jessica. One look and the grown-ups knew something had happened. Miss Bilgore stared at the class, waiting for someone to tell her.

In the end, it was Louisa who told the story, and that was a good thing, too. Because Louisa was still so excited, it was impossible for anybody to be angry with her — or with anybody else. After all, the piglets were all safely back in the pen. By the time Louisa finished talking, even the grown-ups were laughing at what had happened.

Then, it was nearly time to go. By asking the bus driver to help, they took one more picture of everybody — including Mr. and Mrs. Akers, Partner, Mildred, and all of her piglets. Everybody was smiling. Everybody meant it.

Chapter 30

*

The Power of the Press

It didn't take long for word of the piglets' round-up to get around the school. Two fifth graders even asked Brad if the story was true. He told them it was. They didn't seem to believe him.

But they believed him after it came out in the newspaper. Zoe's pictures were really good. They were so good that when Zoe's father showed them to the editor of *The Bulletin*, he decided to print the entire story.

The headline read: ROUND-UP AT AK-ERS ACRES. The pictures told the whole story of the day. First, there was a happy picture of the class and the horse. Then, there was a picture of Jeremy falling down in the pigsty, and the telltale picture of Brad opening the gate.

Next came a photograph of twelve happy piglets running to the field and the whole series of the round-up: Partner shooing piglets, Brad bagging the first one, Michael and Melissa grabbing their pair, Ellie Vanquist carrying the sleepy one, Louisa sitting proudly on Partner and then picking up the piglet from next to the rock. Everything was there and everything was in *The Bulletin* — even the final picture of the class and Partner and the pigs. That was the nicest picture of all.

"Hey, look at this!" Jennie said from behind the newspaper. It was Social Studies time, but what they were really doing was reading *The Bulletin,* which had just arrived. "They called us 'pigpokes'!" Jennie was indignant.

"Instead of 'cowpokes'?" Brad asked.

"I guess so, and I don't like it!"

"Well, if a cowpoke herds cows, then

ROUND-UP AT
AKERS ACRES

I suppose a pigpoke herds pigs — and that's what we did, right?"

"Yes," Jennie admitted. "That's what we did." She looked back at the newspaper. "Oooooh! Here's a picture of me in the tree. It says, 'Jennie Everett masterminded the operation.' Isn't that nice? But there's more. It says here, 'Brad Carter neatly bags a stray piglet.' That's nice, too."

That was when Brad knew for sure that Jennie felt the same way he did about teamwork.

"And look what it says about Louisa!" Excitedly, Jennie read almost the whole story to her class — including everything nice that the story said about everyone, not just about herself. Everyone could share in the fun with Jennie.

The part of the newspaper article that Brad liked the very best was where it explained about Rent a Third Grader and what Miss Bilgore's class was doing for Partner — and why. Brad, and everybody else, was aware of the power of the press. They were all sure this would bring them new business.

And they were right.

At recess, Miss Mortimer, the principal's secretary, asked Brad, Jennie, and Louisa to come to her office to pick up phone messages. There were twenty-eight of them! Twenty-eight people wanted to rent third graders!

"Yippeeeee!" Brad, Jennie, and Louisa yelled together on their way back to the classroom. Quickly, they decided to have everyone in the class call one person back. That left one extra.

"I'll take it," Brad said, grabbing for the last message.

Brad made his calls when he got home from school. The first one was to a woman who needed someone to pull weeds from her lawn. Brad agreed to do that on Saturday. The woman would pay $1.50 an hour. She said it would take about three hours.

Brad got out his pencil. If everybody

in the class got jobs for $1.50 for three hours, they'd earn $121.50, which would be enough to pay for Partner's boarding for two months *and* to pay his parents back for their loan, and still have a little bit left.

It was wonderful news.

But it wasn't as wonderful as his other phone call.

Brad dialed the number.

"Pet's Joy Pet Food Company," a man answered.

Oh, *no!* Brad thought. Somebody else wants to get their hands on Partner!

"Frank Hastrom, please," Brad said, reading the name from the message.

A few seconds later, a deep voice said, "Hello?"

"Mr. Hastrom, this is Brad Carter. You called about Rent a Third Grader at the elementary school, so I'm calling you back. If you want to make dog food out of Partner, too, we won't let you. We're going to protect him as long as he lives, see. We're a team, now, and we will fight you as hard as we fought old Snodgrass!"

"Hold on there, Brad," Mr. Hastrom said, laughing, "I don't want to make Partner into dog food."

"You don't?" Brad said, relieved. But he still wasn't about to trust this guy. "Then what do you want?"

"I want to sell horse feed," Mr. Hastrom said. "And I think you and your classmates can help me."

"We can?"

"I hope so," he said. And then he explained what he wanted.

"*Really?*"

"Really," Mr. Hastrom said.

"I'll have to talk to my committee."

"Of course you do, Brad. Can you call me back tomorrow and let me know?"

"You bet!" Brad said and then hung up the phone. He was happier than he had been since the first day he'd thought about saving Partner.

Chapter 31

The End —
or Is It?

The next day, the classroom was all abuzz. Almost everybody had called someone back yesterday and had made a deal to earn some money. It was very exciting.

But Brad had the most exciting news of all.

"I have an announcement," Brad began. Miss Bilgore invited him to the front of the room. He told the class about speaking to Mr. Hastrom. "His company isn't like HappiPet. At all. He's a really nice man. And here's what he wants. They've just made a new feed that is specially made for older horses, like Partner. When Mr. Hastrom saw the picture of us and Partner in the paper, he decided it was the perfect picture to put on the bags for the feed. He told me he'd never seen a happier horse than Partner. And he said he wants people to know that this food is for horses that get a lot of love. So, the picture shows us loving Partner and that's just what he wants."

"Hey, that's great for us, too," Jennie said. "If we're all on that bag, then everybody who sees it will think of calling us and helping us to earn more money for Partner."

"Maybe, but here's the best news," Brad told her. "In order to pay us for using the picture, Mr. Hastrom said Pet's Joy would pay Mr. Akers' bill every month — for as long as Partner is alive! And he'll get a lifetime supply of nutritious horse feed. He's saved! We've done it!"

At first, everybody was too surprised to say anything. But then it sunk in and they started yelling and cheering. They couldn't believe it. They'd won. And they'd done it all by themselves.

Partner was absolutely guaranteed to have a happy, long life — and he could have as much Pet's Joy Senior Mix Horse Feed as he could eat.

Brad sat down in his chair, glowing with pride. A lot of the kids came over to congratulate him.

"But it's not me, don't you see?" he asked. "It's *us*. We did it. Our committee — our class — our team. We all won. But most of all, Partner won. Isn't it wonderful?"

Brad felt a kind of glowing warmth of happiness and pride — in himself and in his classmates — even Jennie and Louisa. No, he told himself, *especially* Jennie and Louisa.

Brad was ready to make a list of things he wanted to think about. It included Partner. It included Mr. Costello's baseball-card collection. And it included the job he would do on Saturday.

Now there was an interesting thought. The way he'd figured it, within a week or so, the class would have earned more than a hundred dollars.

What would they do with it? He thought about that.

"Brad Carter! Are you going to join us today?" That was Miss Bilgore speaking.

"Yes, Miss Bilgore," he said sheepishly. "I'm sorry. My mind was on something else."

"I guess I can understand that," she said, smiling. "You really had something to think about. But I had something to think about, too. And I owe you an apology."

"You do?"

"Yes, I do. I was looking through my lesson plans at lunchtime and I suddenly realized that you never had a chance to do your community report. I know you have all the material. It's there in your cubby. Why don't you present it now?"

That was the last thing in the world

he'd expected to hear. Ever. He remembered the report. The monkey wrench. The air filter. The instruction manual.

He started to stand up and get the bag from his cubby. His mind was racing.

"You know, Miss Bilgore," he said. "Because of the newspaper story, Rent a Third Grader is going to make a lot of money. Since Partner won't need it, maybe there's another way to use the money in the community."

"Gee, Brad," she said. "That's an interesting idea. Does anybody have any ideas for the money?"

Three hands went up. Brad sat back down at his desk. There would be no report on garages today, he thought happily.

LITTLE  APPLE®

Here are some of our favorite Little Apples.

*Once you take a bite out of a
Little Apple book—you'll want to
read more!*

**Books
for Kids
with BIG
Appetites!**

❏ NA45899-X **Amber Brown Is Not a Crayon**
Paula Danziger **$2.99**

❏ NA42833-0 **Catwings** Ursula K. LeGuin **$3.50**

❏ NA42832-2 **Catwings Return** Ursula K. LeGuin **$3.50**

❏ NA41821-1 **Class Clown** Johanna Hurwitz **$3.50**

❏ NA42400-9 **Five True Horse Stories** Margaret Davidson **$3.50**

❏ NA42401-7 **Five True Dog Stories** Margaret Davidson **$3.50**

❏ NA43868-9 **The Haunting of Grade Three**
Grace Maccarone **$3.50**

❏ NA40966-2 **Rent a Third Grader** B.B. Hiller **$3.50**

❏ NA41944-7 **The Return of the Third Grade Ghost Hunters**
Grace Maccarone **$2.99**

❏ NA47463-4 **Second Grade Friends** Miriam Cohen **$3.50**

❏ NA45729-2 **Striped Ice Cream** Joan M. Lexau **$3.50**

Available wherever you buy books...or use the coupon below.

- -

SCHOLASTIC INC., P.O. Box 7502, 2931 East McCarty Street, Jefferson City, MO 65102

Please send me the books I have checked above. I am enclosing $ _____ (please add
$2.00 to cover shipping and handling). Send check or money order—no cash or C.O.D.s
please.

Name_____

Address_____

City_____**State/Zip**_____

Please allow four to six weeks for delivery. Offer good in the U.S.A. only. Sorry, mail orders are not
available to residents of Canada. Prices subject to change.   LAP198

Creepy, weird, wacky and
funny things happen to
the Bailey School Kids!™
Collect and read them all!

The Adventures of THE BAILEY SCHOOL KIDS®

❏ BAS43411-X	#1	Vampires Don't Wear Polka Dots $3.99
❏ BAS44061-6	#2	Werewolves Don't Go to Summer Camp $3.99
❏ BAS44477-8	#3	Santa Claus Doesn't Mop Floors $3.99
❏ BAS44822-6	#4	Leprechauns Don't Play Basketball $3.99
❏ BAS45854-X	#5	Ghosts Don't Eat Potato Chips $3.99
❏ BAS47071-X	#6	Frankenstein Doesn't Plant Petunias $3.99
❏ BAS47070-1	#7	Aliens Don't Wear Braces $3.99
❏ BAS47297-6	#8	Genies Don't Ride Bicycles $3.99
❏ BAS47298-X	#9	Pirates Don't Wear Pink Sunglasses $3.99
❏ BAS48112-6	#10	Witches Don't Do Backflips $3.99
❏ BAS48113-4	#11	Skeletons Don't Play Tubas $3.99
❏ BAS48114-2	#12	Cupid Doesn't Flip Hamburgers $3.99
❏ BAS48115-0	#13	Gremlins Don't Chew Bubble Gum $3.99
❏ BAS22635-5	#14	Monsters Don't Scuba Dive $3.99
❏ BAS22636-3	#15	Zombies Don't Play Soccer $3.99
❏ BAS22638-X	#16	Dracula Doesn't Drink Lemonade $3.99
❏ BAS22637-1	#17	Elves Don't Wear Hard Hats $3.99
❏ BAS50960-8	#18	Martians Don't Take Temperatures $3.99
❏ BAS50961-6	#19	Gargoyles Don't Drive School Buses $3.99
❏ BAS50962-4	#20	Wizards Don't Need Computers $3.99
❏ BAS22639-8	#21	Mummies Don't Coach Softball $3.99
❏ BAS84886-0	#22	Cyclops Doesn't Roller-Skate $3.99
❏ BAS84902-6	#23	Angels Don't Know Karate $3.99
❏ BAS84904-2	#24	Dragons Don't Cook Pizza $3.99
❏ BAS84905-0	#25	Bigfoot Doesn't Square Dance $3.99
❏ BAS84906-9	#26	Mermaids Don't Run Track $3.99
❏ BAS25701-3	#27	Bogeymen Don't Play Football $3.99
❏ BAS25783-8	#28	Unicorns Don't Give Sleigh Rides $3.99
❏ BAS25804-4	#29	Knights Don't Teach Piano $3.99
❏ BAS25809-5	#30	Hercules Doesn't Pull Teeth $3.99
❏ BAS25819-2	#31	Ghouls Don't Scoop Ice Cream $3.99
❏ BAS18982-4	#32	Phantoms Don't Drive Sports Cars $3.99
❏ BAS18983-2	#33	Giants Don't Go Snowboarding $3.99
❏ BAS99552-9		Bailey School Kids Joke Book $3.99
❏ BAS88134-5		Bailey School Kids Super Special #1:
		Mrs. Jeepers Is Missing! $4.99
❏ BAS21243-5		Bailey School Kids Super Special #2:
		Mrs. Jeepers' Batty Vacation $4.99
❏ BAS11712-2		Bailey School Kids Super Special #3:
		Mrs. Jeepers' Secret Cave $4.99

Available wherever you buy books, or use this order form

Scholastic Inc., P.O. Box 7502, Jefferson City, MO 65102

Please send me the books I have checked above. I am enclosing $_____ (please add $2.00 to cover shipping and handling). Send check or money order — no cash or C.O.D.s please.

Name _____

Address _____

City _____ State/Zip _____

Please allow four to six weeks for delivery. Offer good in the U.S. only. Sorry, mail orders are not available to residents of Canada. Prices subject to change.   BSK498